D0731805

The Blue Dolphin

A WWII Novel

KATHRYN GAUCI

First published in 2021 by Ebony Publishing

ISBN: 9780648714422

Copyright © Kathryn Gauci 2021

This novel is a work of fiction based on real events. Except for those names and institutions in the public domain, all the characters and organisations mentioned are either a product of the author's imagination or, if real, used fictitiously without any intent to describe actual conduct. Any resemblance to real persons, living or dead, is entirely co-incidental.

Clytemnestra

For me, the tears that welled like spring are dry.
I have no tears to spare.
I'd watch till late at night, my eyes still burn,
I sobbed the torch I lit for you alone.

I never let it die...but in my dreams
the high thin wail of a gnat would rouse me,
piercing like a trumpet — I could see you suffer more than all
the hours that slept with me could ever bear.

From Agamemnon (in The Oresteia)
Aeschylus (525-456 B.C.)

Contents

Chapter 1

JUNE 1944

THE SUN WAS quickly slipping over the horizon into the Aegean Sea like a rich red fireball falling from heaven. In the final minutes of its descent, the water resembled a great expanse of undulating molten lava. Within minutes it was gone, pulled into the underworld by the sea gods, leaving behind an inky blue vastness over which now hung a beautiful silver moon. This was the time of day Nefeli loved the most: the time when she could reflect on the events of the day. These days the Blue Dolphin taverna was lucky to have more than a handful of patrons, and rarely in the evening. With money scarce, she was thankful to the fishermen who called by in the morning with their fresh catch and offered her a choice of fish. In exchange, she would cook them a meal. Nefeli was an excellent cook and every dish was a feast, particularly her *kakavia* — fisherman's soup — which she simmered in her special three-legged tripod cooking pot. With a war on, fish and simple dishes made from dried peas, beans and chickpeas were often the only things on the menu. Sometimes there would be vegetable dishes, especially if they came from her garden, or she managed to exchange the fish for a few vegetables from the villagers in Chora some three kilometres away on the other side of the island. Occasionally there would even be lamb, but only on festive occasions. It was the *kakavia,* made with the smallest fish, that the fishermen favoured the most. Seasoned with olive oil, onions, and saffron, it was hard to beat.

Tonight had been a special occasion and she made twice the amount, even adding a few clams and prawns to it. Her guests complemented her cooking by mopping their dishes clean with their bread. When the evening drew to a close, she bid goodbye to her guests on the terrace and returned inside to clean up. It was getting late and she needed to get back home to her young daughter. From the taverna window, she could see the villagers' lanterns flickering like fireflies as they wound their way along the stony track up the mountainside towards Chora. It was the island's main village, and unless you counted the small cluster of houses around Mikrolimano, the small harbour on the other side of the island, it was the only village. By mule, it would take them half an hour to reach their destination. In no time at all, the lights disappeared behind the rocks.

Nefeli picked up the empty glasses and dishes from the table and washed them ready for the next day. Before leaving, she gave the tables a good wipe, swept the floor and closed the deep blue shutters over the windows. Outside on the terrace, she lit her lantern and as she locked the taverna door she felt a slight gust of wind. It had been a beautiful hot summer's day and the sea looked calm but the fishermen warned her earlier that day that a storm was expected.

'It's going to be a violent one,' Socrates had said, as he sat mending his nets on the beach. 'Zeus himself is about to unleash his fury and I fear that this time, he will call on all the other weather gods. It's because of the war.'

Socrates had been a fisherman all his life and had survived many storms. He was a devout Christian Orthodox man and, like all fishermen, was extremely superstitious. When it came to the sea, he even believed in the power of the old Greek gods too: hedging his bets as he called it. His red and white wooden fishing boat, which he'd named *Zephyr*, had a cobalt blue eye painted next to the name to ward off the *mati*, and his pockets were always filled with amulets and charms. As if that wasn't enough, he spat on his nets three times to ensure a good catch before heading out to sea. *Ftou. Ftou. Ftou.* One way or another, Socrates, now in his late sixties, had managed to stave off the curse of the evil eye and the anger of the gods longer than many of his fellow fisherman, some of whom had been friends and family. The last one to die was a cousin whose boat was blown to smithereens when it hit a German mine — an all too common occurrence since the Italians and Germans had occupied the islands. Now Socrates added war to his long list of evils of being out at sea.

Nefeli wore a voluminous, scarlet calf-length skirt with a simple white cotton blouse that slipped easily off her olive-skinned shoulders, and the sudden gust sent a chill through her body. Unsure of whether Socrates' prediction about the fury of the gods was about to come true, she went back into the taverna

9

and fetched her black widow's shawl just in case the wind whipped up even more. She picked up the lantern, walked over to her mule, Agamemnon, and placed a container of leftover *kakavia* and bread in the panniers, tugged on the rein, and set off along the coastal track towards home. A small but wiry and intelligent animal, Agamemnon was Nefeli's constant companion and she rarely went anywhere on the island without him. As a rule, she rode him, especially when she was tired, but today she had chosen to walk instead. The walk from her house to the taverna was just over a kilometre away and the sandy path meandered along the sea front, skirting small coves and several rocky outcrops with hidden caves used by smugglers. The soft tinkling sound of the bell around Agamemnon's neck, combined with the gentle sound of the waves rolling in and out of the rocks was hypnotic. On one side she had a clear view of the sea, glistening like shimmering indigo silk in the moonlight, and on the other side, the island, which was now a series of undulating dark and mysterious silhouettes. Thankfully both she and Agamemnon knew the way home by heart. It was a path she had trodden ever since she had married Yianni, nine years ago.

The day they married and he took her from her home in Chora to his tiny house by the sea was the happiest day of her life. A year later, she gave birth to her daughter, Georgia, and their happiness was complete. They tried for a son but that was not to be. Their idyllic life soon came to an abrupt end with the Italian invasion of Greece from Albania on October 28, 1940. Yianni signed up immediately to fight for his country. She would never see him again. He died somewhere in the Pindus Mountains, north of Epirus. They never found his body and all she received were a few sentences written on military stationery from the Greek High Command in Athens saying that he was missing in action, presumed dead. That day, Nefeli's life changed forever.

She arrived home later than usual, and, except for a lantern burning brightly in the window, the house was almost in darkness. Nefeli tied Agamemnon securely in the outhouse, making sure he had clean water and food before going inside. Georgia was fast asleep, curled up on the kilim in front of the hearth in the kitchen. Nefeli bent over and stroked her forehead gently.

'*Georgaki mou*, I'm back.'

Georgia rubbed her eyes with her fists. 'I'm sorry, Mama. You were longer than usual and I was so tired I fell asleep. What time is it?'

'Almost ten o'clock.'

'Why did your visitors stay so long? Don't they know you come home before sunset?'

Georgia was an inquisitive child and she was aware that her mother had received guests at the taverna that evening as they had discussed what food she would prepare for them. Other than that, Nefeli had told her little else, except to say that it was an important meeting as the guests had ridden all the way from Chora to see her. Nefeli picked her daughter up, carried her into their bedroom and sat her down on the bed. She took off her clothes, slipped a cotton nightdress over her and laid her down, puffing up the pillow and pulling a sheet over her. Georgia was so tired she could barely keep her eyes open.

'Are you coming to bed too, Mama?' she asked, sleepily.

These days they slept together in the same bed. The loss

of her father and the ongoing war had frightened Georgia so much she couldn't sleep alone without having nightmares. As a consequence, Nefeli allowed her to sleep with her in the marital bed. Both mother and daughter needed each other.

Nefeli kissed her daughter's cheek. 'I have something to do first. Try and get some sleep. I won't be long.'

She lit a small candle for her and put it on a shelf in a recess in the wall near the bed and returned to the kitchen. Nefeli's house was typical of most other small island houses: whitewashed dry-stone walls with colourful doors and windows in a deep shade of blue. But unlike many, which were single-roomed, she had two rooms: a kitchen which doubled as a living room and another, an antechamber with a sleeping area where she kept her dowry chest, a small wardrobe, and the marital bed which was set in a recess. The antechamber was divided from the main room by a large archway, decorated with a border of incised stonework. The main room was where they spent all their time and, although the layout was chiefly utilitarian, there were elements of decoration that gave the house its own unique character.

When Yianni built the Blue Dolphin taverna, he built the house at the same time and lived there alone until the day of his wedding. The day after Nefeli accepted his proposal of marriage, as a gesture of his love and commitment, he commissioned an itinerant icon painter from the island of Lesbos, who also painted the interiors of homes, to add a few decorative touches to give the house more charm. The painter's first job was to decorate the main wall around the fireplace. Knowing that Yianni owned the taverna, he painted images of dolphins and the head of Poseidon amid a landscape of classical garlands interspersed with shells and roses. The colours were all hand-mixed from a limited assortment of pigments in shades of blue, ochre, grey, and oxide reds. It was certainly an unusual blend of motifs, and rather naïve, but the artist did have a certain flair and Yianni was so taken with the effect that he asked him to paint another frieze, this time around a large recess which held a divan. The divan was smaller than the marital bed and used both as a sofa and a bed. Again, he painted more garlands and rosettes but this time added a small seascape dotted with caiques over the top of the recess. If one looked closely, they could see his name inscribed in one of the garlands — Yiannakos of Mytilene. When Nefeli first laid eyes on the paintings she thought them most charming, commenting that the colours would complement her embroidered cloths, many of which had red as the main colour. In the soft, flickering glow of the lantern light, the motifs came alive — hypnotic and soothing — especially after a long day's hard work.

Nefeli made herself a soothing warm drink of mountain herbs, added a spoonful of honey, and sat on the soft cushion in the window seat, staring out at the inky blue sea. So far Socrates' dire prediction about the fury of the gods had not come to pass. The sudden gust of wind she'd felt earlier had gone away and the sea appeared calm. Her thoughts drifted back to the conversation with her guests at the Blue Dolphin. The meeting had not altogether come as a surprise. In fact she'd expected it long before now, but when it did come, she wasn't ready for it. Her mind was in turmoil and she needed time to think over their proposal.

'It's been almost four years now, Nefeli,' Kyria Eleni said. 'The time for grieving is over. You are still young and beautiful and you must find yourself another husband.' The others around the table agreed with her. 'Besides, you have the child to think of. She needs a father.'

'And brothers and sisters,' Kyria Kalliope added.

The villagers realised it was a difficult thing to talk about as Yianni and Nefeli's marriage had been one of love rather than a proposal by the matchmakers. When he was killed, she grieved for months on end until they thought she was losing her mind. If it had not been for the fact that she had a young daughter and the responsibility of looking after the taverna, they feared she would have killed herself. But the villagers were practical. With a war on, they considered it too difficult for a young woman like Nefeli to look after a child and run a taverna at the same time. Nefeli on the other hand, wanted to keep busy. She and Yianni had run the taverna together and knowing that he had left it in her care gave her the strength to carry on.

Behind her back, the villagers met together to see what they could do about the situation. Nefeli was not unaware of that fact but until now, chose to ignore them.

'Yianni was a brave *palikari*,' Kyria Kalliope said. 'He was a credit to us all. He died for Greece but he wouldn't want you to spend the rest of your life alone, would he? Think about it.'

Nefeli listened, taking it all in while plying them with wine and more *kakavia*. This was the first time they'd actually confronted her about her "unfortunate situation" as they referred to it, and she knew it wouldn't be the last. Many of these villagers were like a dog with a bone and they would beat her down until she remarried. It was either that or they would ostracize her and label her in ways she did not care to think about. She'd seen it before. It was the last comment that Kyria Angeliki said which upset her the most.

'Look at yourself, Nefeli. You are beautiful, but with your blouse off your shoulders — like now.' Kyria Angeliki waved her hands up and down and curled her mouth in contempt to stress her point. 'For the first few years you were a respectful widow and wore black. Now, you show far too much flesh. Our men are starting to look at you with lascivious eyes. They are like bees attracted to honey. Do you want people to give you the evil eye? You will be labelled a fallen women and have men committing sins that could have been avoided.'

Kyria Angeliki worked herself up into such a state she picked up her napkin and fanned herself. The oppressive heat had got to them all. Nefeli caught sight of herself in the mirror. Her skin glistened with sweat. She ran her hand through her long dark hair and sighed heavily. *They will water me with poison,* she thought to herself.

'I work hard all day: the weather is unbearable, and I can't see the point of suffocating in more clothes.' She glanced around the table at the three women, all of them clad from head to toe in heavy dark-coloured clothing which was not at all flattering. They were jealous: that's what it was. Maybe it was their own men that looked at her lasciviously as they put it. *I like to feel the sea air on my skin* she thought to herself, but these women wouldn't understand. She was a free spirit. Yianni understood her. He wouldn't want her to dress in black for the rest of her life, but he wasn't here to defend her now.

'At least think about it,' Kyria Eleni said, trying to diffuse the tension in the room.

15

Nefeli promised to give it some thought. For the moment that would keep them quiet, but they would be back, and next time they would be more forceful.

She heard a soft voice and turned to see Georgia standing in the archway.

'Mama, please come to bed. I can't sleep.'

Nefeli pulled herself together. 'I'm sorry, my little one. I'm coming.'

She took her daughter's hand, turned out the lantern and went to bed. Georgia curled up in her mother's arms and within minutes was fast asleep. Nefeli said her nightly prayer to the icon of the Virgin hanging on the wall over the bed, adding that she hoped she would come to her aid and help her make the right decision. Before long, she too drifted into a deep sleep.

Chapter 2

NEFELI WAS STILL asleep when she felt Georgia tugging the sheet.

'Mama, wake up. You're late.'

Nefeli sat up with a start. 'Goodness! What time is it?'

'Eight o'clock. You were so tired I didn't want to wake you up before. I've prepared breakfast.'

Nefeli took a quick wash, dressed in the same red skirt she'd worn the day before and a different white blouse, this time one with puff sleeves with a V-neck drawstring, and sat down to eat her food. A small hand-painted jug filled with freshly picked wildflowers had thoughtfully been placed on the table, and there were hard-boiled eggs, goat's cheese, honey, and rusks — all of which were their own produce.

'What a treat my little one, I am so lucky to have such a good daughter.'

Georgia sat down to eat with her. 'I watched the way you laid out the tables at the taverna. You taught me how to make things look attractive. Don't you remember? You said that if the table looks inviting, then the food will be twice as delicious.'

Nefeli laughed. Her daughter was a quick learner. 'Your father would be very proud of you, *agapi mou.*'

After they'd finished, Georgia fetched Agamemnon and together they filled the panniers with food to take to the taverna. The Blue Dolphin had its own oven, but with few customers because of the war, Nefeli and Georgia usually did the baking in the outdoor oven at home. Georgia may have only been eight years old, but she was already skilled in many household chores. She knew how to make dough and shape it into loaves, how to light the outdoor oven and wait until the fire reached the correct temperature before slipping the loaves inside on the long wooden paddle. She also helped her mother prepare stuffed vegetables and could bake her favourite biscuits –koulourakia — traditionally considered to be Easter cookies but which they cooked as their own special treat each week. When she wasn't preparing food, she helped to keep the house spick and span, feeding the chickens and three goats, watering the vegetables, and helping with the olive harvest. The chores were never-ending. As if that wasn't enough, she walked to the schoolhouse in Chora or studied with her mother either at home or in the taverna. There was little time to play: the war had stolen her childhood.

Even though the Italians had capitulated, the war showed no sign of ending yet, and the Germans were making life even more difficult for everyone. It was hard to get food unless you produced it yourself, and there were sea battles which could be heard miles away, airplanes that harassed the fishermen and dropped bombs on the islands, and frequent surprise visits by the Germans to try and catch the *andartes* or anyone attempting to escape to Turkey. During the last few months, Georgia often made the long journey to the village school only to find it closed. When this happened, she returned to the Blue Dolphin taverna and continued her studies there. Nefeli was consumed with guilt at her daughter's plight, yet there was little she could do except send her to an orphanage on the mainland as some other families did, and that was out of the question.

'*Georgaki mou*, I want to ask you something,' Nefeli said just as she was about to leave. 'How would you feel about having another father? What I mean to say is, how would you feel if I got married again?'

Georgia's happy smile faded. 'Why, Mama? Aren't we happy as we are?'

The tears welled up in her daughter's eyes and she ran inside the house and threw herself on the bed. Nefeli hurried after her.

'My darling, you and I have something no-one else will ever share. We are one, but sometimes I worry about you. You have so much to do for someone so young.' She stroked her face gently. 'I'm only thinking about you.'

The look in Georgia's eyes told her she wasn't sure if that was altogether true.

'Mama, I'm not silly you know. I've heard the whispers in the village: people saying it was time "widow Nefeli" married again.'

Nefeli hated hearing this. How could people be so cruel to say such things when her daughter could hear? Maybe that was what they wanted? Maybe they thought Georgia might encourage her to remarry. It was all part of their grand plan. What a conniving lot they were.

'It was just a question, my darling. I would never do anything unless you agreed. As I said, we are one. Now give me a kiss. I must get going or there will be no fish left for me.'

Georgia threw her arms around her mother and hugged her. '*S'agapo*, Mama.'

'And I love you too, my little one.'

Socrates was sitting on the shore mending his nets when Nefeli arrived at the taverna. Made of linen, his nets had to be carefully cleaned and dried each day or they would rot and wear out. Weights consisting of small pieces of stone with holes drilled in them were fastened to the bottom of the nets. Nefeli thought much of a fisherman's life seemed to be spent mending their nets as it took up so much time. She wondered how they had the patience.

'I was beginning to wonder where you'd got to,' Socrates said, attaching the weights to an area he'd just repaired. 'I managed to save you some fish: one grey mullet, two calamari and a few sardines. The rest of the catch has been taken.'

Nefeli was grateful for anything she could get, and told him so.

'By the way, what happened to your prophecy about the storm? There was a slight sea breeze for less than half an hour and then it died down. It's not like you to be wrong.'

He threw her a stern look as he threaded the weights. 'He's playing with us. Maybe tonight, but mark my words, when Zeus is angry, Charon will be out looking for the dead and ferrying them to the underworld.'

Nefeli knew him better than to argue. She thanked him for the fish and continued to the steps that led to the taverna. Socrates was full of odd sayings and prophecies, but today she had enough on her mind without worrying about Charon taking souls into the underworld. The day was already warming up and she set out a couple of tables on the terrace. On each one she placed a small container of red geraniums: a homely touch that set off the cobalt blue of the tables and chairs perfectly.

The taverna had been in this remote part of the island for years and was in a rundown state when Yianni took it over. He patched up the walls, painted the outside a deep shade of ochre and the inside white, and added an open-air terrace with a rush matting roof which looked out towards the islands of Kos and Astypalaia. Further south were the islands of Nikia, Tilos and Rhodes. He had just got it into shape and was starting to run a thriving business when the war began. Rather than sell it or leave it to fall into disrepair, Nefeli took it over, even though she had a young child. Yianni had put his heart and soul into the Blue Dolphin and she wasn't going to let it go to rack and ruin again. Besides, there was little else to do. The only options were to sell it for less than it was worth because of the war, or get married in order to keep what little money there was coming in. Now the latter was rearing its ugly head again.

Sweeping the terrace, she saw a small boat heading towards them. Hoping it might be bringing a few customers, she put the broom away and tidied herself up. As the boat neared, she heard Socrates call out to them. Four men got out and pulled the boat up on the shore not far from his caique. The men were *andartes* from her island and she recognized them instantly. They chatted with Socrates for a while and then headed towards the taverna.

'*Kalimera,* Kyria Nefeli,' the taller one of the four said.

21

'*Kalimera*, Michalis. I haven't seen you for a few days,' she replied. 'What have you been up to?'

'Hunting down the Germans! They're harder to eliminate than the Italians.'

The way he said eliminate made her shudder. These men were young, but they were ruthless.

'What have you got for us today?' another asked. 'We've had a long night and we're famished.'

Nefeli offered to grill some of the sardines that Socrates had given her earlier. 'I have stuffed tomatoes and *fava* too: how does that sound?'

Stratos, the youngest of the group, rubbed his stomach heartily. 'Perfect.'

They propped their rifles against the wall and sat at a table on the terrace while she went inside to fetch a carafe of red wine from Samos. Nefeli had known these men all their lives. Three were from Chora, the other from the far side of the island near Mikrolimano. They joined the *andartes* soon after the Germans marched into Greece to come to the aid of the Italians in 1941. These days, many of the young and middle-aged men spent most of their time evading the Germans, who regularly raided the islands. Except for collaborators, many Greeks worked in one way or another against the Axis forces, hiding men and escapees fleeing to Turkey. Sometimes the islanders were severely punished and morale quickly dissipated, and at times it felt as if they would never be free again. Michalis was Yianni's best friend. They'd grown up together and he was their *koumbaros* when they married. When Yianni left to fight in 1940, he asked Michalis to keep an eye out for Nefeli and Georgia, but these days Michalis and his friends had grown more used to spending their days and nights in one of the many caves that dotted the shoreline of the Aegean Islands. Venturing home was hazardous, as you never knew who would go running off to inform the Germans to earn themselves some extra money. While she prepared their food, she listened through the open window to their conversation about the situation of the war.

Nefeli's island was barely a rocky outcrop in the Dodecanese Islands in the south-eastern Aegean. At the beginning of the war, the islands came under Italian control as part of the Axis agreement, but in reality, they had been under Italian control since the Italo-Turkish War in 1911. Being strategically well-placed between Greece and Turkey, everyone wanted a slice of them, including the Allies. The largest of the islands was Rhodes, a place Nefeli had been to only twice in her life, but which was now a major military and aerial base. Then there was the island of Leros because of its deep-water port of Portolago. After the defeat of the Axis forces in the North African campaign in May 1943, Winston Churchill, a man most of the islanders had heard about in name only, and mainly from the *andartes,* set his eyes on taking the Dodecanese Islands. Michalis told her that if they could capture the Dodecanese and Crete, they could apply pressure on neutral Turkey to join the war and allow Allied ships access through the Dardanelles. By the end of January 1943, plans were in place for a direct attack on Rhodes and Karpathos with three infantry divisions, an armoured brigade, and support units. The main problem faced by the Allies was countering the strength of *Fliegerkorps* X of the Luftwaffe, particularly in Crete, because of a lack of air cover.

When the islanders got wind of an impending invasion, they tried to help the Allies as much as they could, but to no avail. Michalis said he feared their losses would be in vain as he had heard that the Americans were sceptical about the operation and the Allied invasion of Sicily now took precedence. Even so, the men wanted to fight. With the announcement of the surrender of Italy in September 1943, the Italian garrisons on most of the Dodecanese Islands either wanted to change sides and fight with the Allies or go home. Like the Greeks, they'd had enough of war. The problem was that the Germans were ready for this and rushed many of their forces, mainly based in mainland Greece, to many of the islands to maintain control. For months, battles raged throughout the islands from Kalymnos, Leros, Samos, to Rhodes, but the Allies were no match for the Germans. Nefeli watched the Luftwaffe battle it out in the Aegean skies against RAF spitfires, joined by the South African Air Force. Stories abounded of Battalions and Parachute Regiments, of Infantry Brigades coming from Malta along with special boat services together with their own Greek Sacred Band, until in the end no-one knew what to believe. The fact that their own fighting force, which had been formed by the government in exile in Egypt and fought alongside the SAS in the Western Desert, was now fighting alongside the Allies, had at first filled the islanders with hope, but after months of bloodshed, only the island of Kastellorizo remained in Allied hands. Their hopes were dashed. All this and they were in a worse situation than before: the Germans were digging in.

Michalis confided in Nefeli one day over ouzo and octopus, that the plans to retake the islands were a complete fiasco. Badly conceived and executed from the beginning, the islanders lost many men and every day there was a funeral held for the brave inhabitants on every island. It was an ongoing struggle and no-one knew what to expect next. Wreckage from downed aircraft and ships blown out of the water washed up on a daily basis along the shoreline, along with bodies, many in such a bad state of decomposition that neither side knew who they belonged to. Even Socrates complained about the amount of spilled fuel and wreckage that affected his fishing. The only good thing for the fishermen was that explosions at sea killed the fish making them float to the surface and easy to net. It did take the edge off eating the fish when you knew how it was netted, but times were hard and the villagers were grateful for what they could get so all gruesome thoughts were momentarily put aside to enjoy a meal.

All this added to Georgia's anxiety. There was nothing Nefeli could do to stop her daughter seeing planes shot out of the sky or coming across wreckage and dead bodies when she played on the beach or went to catch shellfish. It was little wonder the child had nightmares.

Nefeli took the sardines off the grill and arranged them neatly on a bed of vine leaves around which she placed quartered lemons. She put them on the tray alongside the stuffed tomatoes and *fava*, which was drizzled with a generous amount of olive oil and a last minute addition of diced onion and chopped parsley, and took them outside. The delicate aromas wafted through the window and made the men even hungrier. When she placed the food on the table, their eyes lit up and big smiles appeared on their faces.

'Your dishes are always mouth-watering,' Pavlos said. 'The surest way to a man's heart is through a woman's cooking. Yianni was a lucky man.' He squeezed lemon juice over the sardines and picked one up with his fingers. 'Every dish you cook is irresistible; I could easily become addicted to your food.' He threw her a cheeky smile. 'I should marry you myself and I would never go hungry again.'

In light of the previous evening's conversation, Nefeli's face reddened.

'Now look what you've done, you imbecile,' Michalis said, chastising him playfully. 'You've embarrassed her.' Seeing that Nefeli wasn't smiling, he apologised on behalf of his friend. 'Take no notice, he's in a happy mood that's all — and tired. We killed a boatload of Germans last night and he's letting off steam.'

Nefeli said it was fine: she wasn't offended and took it in the spirit it was intended. The men were usually well-behaved and she knew their undercover work gave them a rush of adrenalin. Yet when she went back inside, she flung her teatowel on the table and let out a deep sigh. Pavlos' comment had brought the subject of marriage to the fore again. Listening to their chatter and laughter outside, she wondered if any of them were on the list of eligible bachelors the village women had in mind for her. Only one of them was married — Dimitri — the quiet one who lived on the other side of the island and he had two children. She thought about the others. Michalis was a similar age to Yianni, thirty-three — too old to be a bachelor by village standards. Perhaps they'd got into his ear too. All the same, she couldn't believe Michalis was the sort of man who would be party to the old women's conniving gossip and devious plotting. He would see through them straight way. Then there was Stratos who was about the same age as she was — twenty-seven. The fourth one was Pavlos, the youngest of the group. He was twenty-two, the right age the villagers thought for a man to find himself a bride. In the end, Nefeli didn't think any of them would be a party to the old women's marriage plans. They had too much on their mind fighting the Germans. Not only that, but they had shown her great respect after Yianni died, Michalis in particular. No-one harassed her and she felt safe with them. It was one or two of the older men in Chora — the ones married to women who bore them children and then preferred stuffing marrows and baking biscuits to satisfying their husband's sexual desires — that worried her the most. They were the ones who threw her lascivious glances over their *tavli* and cards whenever she passed them sitting outside the *kafeneia*. Their own women no longer had a need for them, except as a provider, but it didn't stop them being jealous. She was always careful to cover herself with a headscarf whenever she went there but she was well aware of the men's eyes undressing and devouring her as she passed. Occasionally she would hear a hiss or a crude remark muttered under their breath and tried hard to ignore it, but it wasn't easy. She was becoming a recluse and it wasn't good. It wasn't good for Georgia either. It wouldn't be the first time they had turned a child against her own mother.

She pulled herself together and went outside to fill up their wine carafe.

'Is there anything else I can get you?' she asked. 'I have rizogalo, if you'd like a desert. I made it yesterday.'

The men's eyes lit up. This time Pavlos didn't utter a word. Nefeli smiled. 'It's okay,' she said to him, 'you haven't offended me.'

She went inside and took four glasses of rice pudding from the meat safe. Thankfully the safe was in a well-ventilated area to allow for air flow, and the rice pudding was lovely and cool. She sprinkled a little cinnamon on top and gave them one each. The scent of lemon and cinnamon filled the air.

'Delicious,' Michalis said, after savouring the first bite. He smacked his lips together and kissed his fingers, flicking them open with a flourish. 'Simply delicious.'

Nefeli pulled up a chair and joined them. She wanted to know what was going on with the war, in particular the sinking of the SS *Tanai*, a Greek-owned cargo ship that was requisitioned by the Germans earlier in the war.

'She was torpedoed by a Royal Navy submarine and sunk off the port of Heraklion on June 9, two days ago. Several hundreds of deported Cretan Jews, Christians, mostly linked to the Resistance, and Italian POWs were aboard,' Michalis replied. 'The number of casualties varies depending on the source, but we estimate that at least five hundred perished.'

'That boat was bad luck,' Stratos said. 'It was sunk by the Luftwaffe earlier in the war and then repaired. It should have been left alone.'

'Anything else?' Nefeli asked. 'Did your night-time escapades net any fish?'

This time Nefeli was referring to issues of a more local nature: guns, explosives, etc.

'Our sources in Kos told us a German ship is leaving tonight. There are plans to attack it. We'll see how it plays out. We've also managed to acquire a few more guns and explosives from a parachute drop by the RAF near an island near the Turkish coast.' Michalis glanced towards the rocks. 'Can we store them in the cave where you keep Yianni's old boat?'

The fishing boat they were using that day belonged to Dimitri and was much larger than Socrates' tiny caique. Dimitri was a carpenter by trade and together they'd managed to fit it out with a double hold to conceal weapons. It was even big enough to hide two people which they'd done from time to time when helping escapees pass through the various escape networks to Turkey. The German takeover of the Dodecanese now meant that Jewish people in particular, were no longer safe and neither was the Resistance. The Italians had been easy to bribe: the Germans were a different matter. They were ruthless in their searches.

Yianni's old boat was a small caique, similar to the one Socrates had. He'd used it himself for fishing and for transporting goods to and from the nearby islands when the ferry didn't run. Like the taverna, he'd named it the "Blue Dolphin". Since he left to fight the Italians at the beginning of the war, it had been kept in a boathouse less than ten minutes away from the taverna. In reality, it was a small cave hidden in the rocks along the coastline. Rumour had it that it was once used by pirates and Greek sailors evading the Turks during the War of Independence. Even though it was a cave, it was fitted with a padlocked iron gate and the key was kept in the taverna on the wall hidden under a wicker basket. Since his death, the boat had never been used, and was in a state of disrepair.

Nefeli got up to fetch the key for them. Michalis followed her inside.

'We can do it ourselves, you don't have to come,' he said.

'No, it looks like being another quiet day so I'll come with you. I can clean up later.'

They headed down the stone steps to their boat on the beach. Socrates was still there, dozing in the shade of his boat. Dimitri and Pavlos lifted the boards away from the hold and passed the guns and ammunition to Stratos and Michalis. Between them they carried their precious cargo along the sandy cove until they came to a series of rock formations protruding into the sea. From there, they followed a narrow pathway through the rocks which led to the cave. Nefeli unlocked the rusty padlock and drew back the gate which looked more like a series of iron bars to a prison than a gate. The Blue Dolphin caique was tilted to one side on a sandy bed near the rocks. It was only a short walk from the cave to the sea, but the cave was carved into the rock in such a way that it was protected from the elements. It could not be seen from the sea, and the stormy waters that lashed against the rocks hardly penetrated it, which is why Yianni kept the boat there. Now it was a perfect place for the *andartes* to store their weapons.

The men moved a few loose rocks and hid the weapons, carefully replacing the rocks afterwards. Over the past few months, they'd managed to build up quite a hoard, especially since the Italians had left. Some of them were so fed-up with fighting, they'd willingly handed their guns and ammunition to the *andartes*. Securing the gate behind them, they walked back towards the taverna. Just before they parted ways, Nefeli caught Michalis' arm and without the others hearing, asked if she could have a word with him.

'Are you alright? You seem worried about something. In fact I noticed you weren't your usual self today.'

Nefeli lowered her gaze. 'I was thinking of getting married again and I would like your opinion. Am I doing the right thing?'

Michalis looked surprised. 'What's brought this on?' He smiled. 'Those old crones haven't been getting in your ear have they?'

'Well...'

'So that's it! They *have* been at you. I heard some gossip in the village and couldn't believe it.' He lifted her chin towards him in an effort to make her look at him. 'Is it what you want?'

'It may be for the best. Georgia needs a father and... Well, it's hard these days. I wondered what you thought Yianni would think: would he agree?'

Michalis laughed. 'He would want you to do what made you happy, that's what. Where does your heart lie?'

'I'm confused. That's why I wanted to talk with you.'

The other three were already in the boat and Stavros waved to him to get a move on.

'Look, I must go. We've been here too long as it is. Can it wait until tomorrow or the day after?'

Nefeli understood. 'That's fine.'

Michalis squeezed her hand. 'We'll talk then, I promise.'

Nefeli watched him stride across the beach towards the water's edge. 'Good luck,' she shouted out. He turned and waved. Within a matter of minutes, the boat was back at sea, rounding the cove until it disappeared out of sight.

She returned to the taverna, cleaned up the dishes before pouring another glass of wine and sitting outside looking out to sea deep in thought. Her mind wandered back to last night's conversation with the women. Getting married again wasn't what she wanted at all, but life was getting harder by the day. The thing was, who did they have in mind? She knew most of the men in the area and no-one seemed to fit the bill as available except for a few middle-aged widowers with no allure whatsoever. She decided to wait and see what they had to say the next time they met.

With the warm sun on her face and a few glasses of wine, she felt so relaxed she started to doze off. After a few minutes, she heard footsteps approaching. It was Georgia carrying her bag with her schoolbooks. The look on her face told her that the school was closed again

'What happened this time?' Nefeli asked.

'The Germans came to the village and made everyone gather in the square. They wanted to know where the *andartes* were. The people told them there weren't any on the island, but they searched the houses anyway, warning that there would be consequences for anyone lying. "Anyone caught harbouring troublemakers will be shot," they said. That was when the teacher told us to go home.'

Nefeli scooped her daughter up and sat her on her lap. She was only eight but already the word *andartes* was familiar to her, even though she wasn't entirely sure what they did. All she knew was that they were fighting the Germans but never asked in what way.

'They asked me if my family was hiding anyone,' she said, 'and pointed a gun at me.'

'What did you say?' Nefeli was furious that they could intimidate a child like that.

'I said I didn't know what they meant. I only know good people.' She looked at her mother with her big dark eyes. 'It's true, isn't it? We don't know any trouble-makers.'

Nefeli stroked her daughter's hair. 'Of course not, now let's go inside and we'll continue your studies there. Then we'll go home early.'

'Mama, do you think the Germans will search our house too?'

'They might. Who knows? But what will they find — nothing. Don't worry: they'll be gone again soon; you'll see.'

Nefeli was wrong. At that moment a German motor-launch, flying the distinctive horizontal red flag with the black swastika on the white circle, appeared around the rocks. She called out to Socrates who awoke with a start and quickly attended his nets again as six German soldiers accompanied by a man in plain clothes approached him. In the meantime, she ushered Georgia into the taverna and told her to sit at a table with her books and look as though she was studying. When she went back outside they were talking to Socrates but she was too far away to hear what they were saying. They saw her and made their way to the taverna. The plain-clothed man was their Greek translator and he asked if she'd had any male visitors that day. She knew they were probably talking about Michalis, Dimitri, Stratos and Pavlos.

'No,' she answered politely. The men had their machine guns pointed at her. Two went inside to take a look around while another three walked around the back. The last one sat down and, through his Greek interpreter, asked her a few questions. After a few minutes, the German spoke, this time in perfect Greek, albeit with a heavy accent. It was a ruse they used all the time, pretending not to know Greek in case anyone opened their mouth and said the wrong thing. One man on the island had been severely beaten for abusing the Germans to a Greek translator when a German understood what he was saying.

'Are you sure?' he asked. 'It wouldn't be good to lie, you know.'

'Quite sure. What are these people you are looking for supposed to have done?' she asked innocently.

The German wouldn't tell her and the Greek simply repeated it wouldn't be wise to lie. Nefeli was glad she'd cleaned up or the men would be quick to spot the amount of glasses and plates left out. Even so, it didn't stop them checking the rubbish and inspecting the oven and stove for signs of cooking.

'Who has eaten here in the past few hours?' another man asked in German. The Greek translated.

'Only myself and my daughter — and the fisherman who brings me fish.'

The men appeared satisfied and left. Nefeli found herself shaking and sat down to steady her nerves. Socrates came over and said they told him someone had stolen guns from another island. When she asked if he mentioned the men being here earlier, he said no. Nefeli went back inside and comforted Georgia who looked terrified. She gave her a drink of lemonade and sat down, intending to help her with her studies for an hour or so, but after a visit by the Germans it was impossible to concentrate. After a while, Nefeli closed the taverna and they went home. Socrates warned her again to watch for the storm.

'It's definitely coming,' he told her. 'Maybe tonight; tomorrow at the latest.'

Chapter 3

THANKFULLY THE GERMANS did not visit the house, but Nefeli now added the safety of her four friends to her growing list of worries. Were the Germans after them or just targeting all the islanders in general? It was hard to tell. To take her mind off things, she spent the evening preparing dough ready to bake the next morning. After the mounds of dough had been put aside to rise, she relaxed by weaving on her loom. She was making a striped coverlet for the divan. Throughout the winter, she'd spun and dyed the wool herself. It was kept in a large sack next to the loom.

Georgia was sitting on the divan practicing her embroidery: a narrow rectangular piece of cloth which would be used to decorate a shelf. Except for the embroidered pattern on one side where it was to hang, the rest of the cloth was plain. It was made from the finest linen which Nefeli bought from a woman in Chora who specialised in fine weaving: a gift to Georgia for not only excelling at school, but in her embroidery as well. The design consisted of a repeating pattern composed of geometric shapes interspersed with stylised trees in a warm palette of garnet, green and beige. Nefeli was very proud of her.

The cat sat curled up next to her. It was a peaceful, domestic scene that both mother and daughter had become used to, and they sat for a few hours without uttering a word, both engrossed in their own work. At around nine o'clock in the evening, Nefeli saw that Georgia had fallen asleep, her embroidery draped over her chest. Rather than disturb her by waking her up and telling her to go to her bed, she removed the embroidery and covered her with a blanket. Then she went outside to make sure the animals in the outhouse were secure for the evening. There was a chill in the air and a light breeze coming in from the south. One of the goats had given birth around Easter time and the kid was nuzzling against its mother in the hay. Agamemnon stood tethered nearby and, next door, the chickens had settled in their coop. Assured that all was well, she sat for a while on the terrace, breathing in the intoxicating scent of wild herbs and salty sea-air. Having been raised in the confined space of Chora, where the houses were tightly woven in a mesh of winding alleyways with hardly any garden or view at all, Nefeli loved the freedom of her new home. From here she enjoyed the harsh yet beautiful rocky mountain vista and the great expanse of sea with its endless changing colours. It was a simple and hard life, but every day was a pleasure. She stared out to sea, watching the moon slide across the sky. Night after night, she had enjoyed this same view with Yianni. They watched the many boats sail by and wondered where they were going to — an adventure they hoped to take together one day. The war soon put a stop to those dreams. These days it was Georgia who sat with her. She was an inquisitive child and asked a myriad of questions about how things were before the war, and of pirates and exciting sea voyages where people travelled by boat to the ends of the earth. They made a vow to each other. When Georgia finished school and the war was over, they would go to Constantinople together and explore the *polis* where many of the Greeks had once lived.

At that moment the serenity was interrupted by a huge explosion out at sea. It was so loud Georgia woke with a start and came rushing out of the house to find out what happened.

'Mama, what was that noise?'

It was too far out to see what had taken place, but both the sea and sky on the horizon lit up in a fiery red. Nefeli might not have been able to see it, but she could well imagine what had happened. Another German ship had blown up. She'd seen things like this many times over the past year as the Allies fought over the islands, but during the last few months, especially when the Germans retook the islands, things seem to have quietened down a little. She pulled Georgia close. There would be repercussions. There always were. As if that wasn't enough, the earlier soft breeze that had been restraining itself, suddenly started to gather momentum and with it came the soft pitter-patter of rain, which quickly turned into a downpour.

'Hurry! Get inside,' Nefeli said, pushing her daughter into the house before closing the outside shutters. 'There's a storm brewing.'

Within a matter of minutes, the storm turned into a tempest. The heavens opened and the rain came down in torrents, mercilessly lashing the house and making such a terrifying noise they thought the roof would collapse. Deafening thunder claps echoed across the hillside and jagged lightning flashes lit up the sky in brilliant silver streaks. The wind gathered momentum, howling and shrieking around the house, sending slates from the roof crashing to the ground.

Nefeli feared for the animals as the outhouse was a much flimsier construction than the house. She told Georgia to go to bed while she went back outside to try and save them. Wrapped in a heavy coat, she faced the wrath of the storm. As soon as she opened the door, a sharp gust almost pulled the door off its hinges and the howling wind was too wild for her to hear Georgia's pleas for her to stay indoors. Her long dark hair whipped around her face and her clothing became soaked within minutes. She felt feeble against the wind, and mustering up all her strength not to fall over, reached the animals just as the roof blew off the outhouse. Agamemnon was braying noisily, and the goats were wildly trying to free themselves. She had no idea where the chickens had gone as the coop door was open, swinging to and fro on its hinges.

There was no other option but to take the animals into the house but it was impossible to take them all in one go. She decided on the goats first because of the kid, put a rope around their necks and pulled the terrified animals around the side of the house and pushed them inside. Georgia rushed to help, soothing the kid with soft words and cuddles. Next was Agamemnon. He was used to harsh weather, but nothing like this. The thunderclaps terrified him. There was no time to put on the bridle and reins so she slipped the rope over his neck and tugged but he refused to budge, firmly standing his ground in the outhouse and braying loudly. She pulled and shoved to no avail. In the end she grabbed a sodden sack of hay, tipped the contents out, and put the bag over his head, wrapping her arms around his neck and talking to him comfortingly. It soothed him considerably and she was able to guide him out, whispering words of comfort every step of the way. By now, the ground around the house was turning into mud and rivulets of water poured down the mountainside gushing over the rocks. It was a feat of endurance, but she finally managed it. Agamemnon was safe.

While the storm raged, they sat in the kitchen praying that all would be safe. Georgia sat on the bed shivering like a leaf and holding the kid in her arms, and her frightened cat took refuge behind sacks of wool against the loom. The earlier bucolic fragrance of flowers and fresh sea air was now replaced with a peculiar fusion of other, less pleasant smells — animals and fear. While these smells might seem abhorrent to townspeople who no longer lived the rural life, this was normal for Nefeli and Georgia. They had lost count of the times they'd brought the young and the sick and injured animals into the home. Nefeli stripped off her wet clothes and attempted to make a fire but it was useless. Water dripped down the chimney flue and the wind even penetrated the slightest cracks in the house. One of the shutters had come loose and was banging noisily against the window. Throughout the night, they sat huddled together in the kitchen waiting for the tempest to abate. It was harrowing. Socrates *had* been right after all: Zeus had unleashed his fury and the Gods were certainly in a rage, spitting venom on the island. *Was it the fact that we were at war that enraged them,* Nefeli thought to herself. Tonight she feared many poor souls would be ferried into the underworld.

Every now and again, she took a peak out the window where the shutter had come loose. With every flash of lightning she glimpsed the churning sea and saw foaming waves crashing over the rocks. The storm continued for several hours, finally abating just before dawn. For Nefeli, this had been one of the most terrifying storms in living memory and both she and Georgia were utterly exhausted.

With the first light of dawn, Nefeli stepped outside to survey any damage. The sea looked calm and there wasn't a breath of wind at all, yet all around them was devastation. Boulders and rocks had rolled down the hillside, narrowly missing the house, but apart from a few missing tiles, the house had miraculously survived. Only the outhouse lay in a heap, the wooden roof having blown metres across the hillside, smashing into pieces. Pots of herbs and geraniums on the terrace had rolled away and lay smashed against the rocks and several trees had either split in two or crashed to the ground. Even an old olive tree had been uprooted and fallen against the side of the house. Nefeli couldn't believe it and kissed the icon of the Virgin several times, thanking her for keeping them safe.

Georgia searched around for the hens and became distraught when she couldn't find them but Nefeli assured her they would be safe. It wasn't long before she spotted one in the distance and ran to bring it back. Within half an hour, she had caught them all except one and put them in the outhouse with the goats.

Having survived the storm, Nefeli turned her attention to the Blue Dolphin taverna. She knew she'd bolted the shutters before she left and the building was as well-built as the house, but she couldn't be sure what devastation she would find. The taverna was much closer to the beach than the house: maybe it had even been destroyed by the crashing waves. She couldn't leave a traumatised Georgia in the house alone and took her with her.

Nefeli bridled up Agamemnon and because the ground was muddy and slippery, both mother and daughter rode him together to the Blue Dolphin. When they rounded the last bend, the taverna appeared intact, but as they got nearer, they could see debris had collected on the terrace, the rush matting roof over the terrace had blown off, and the two tables and chairs she'd forgotten to put inside were strewn across the sandy beach. She cursed herself for not putting them away as she normally did and blamed the weather for being so deceivingly beautiful at the time. At least they hadn't been washed out to sea.

When she unlocked the taverna door, she was shocked to see how much water had seeped inside from the tidal swells and the floor was still immersed under a few centimetres of water. Thankfully, it was made of stone and there would be little long-term damage. A coat of paint where the water had dampened the whitewashed walls and all would be fine again. Only a large basket of onions and two sacks of beans and flour that had been stored on the floor were ruined. The rest of the food was above the water level and safe. It could have been much worse.

Immediately they began the job of cleaning up. Georgia took a broom and tried to sweep away the water while Nefeli set about shovelling the debris away from the terrace. The light was eerily bright and the sky the palest shade of blue and there was a strange sense of foreboding in it. White-tipped gulls gracefully skimmed the waves landing every now and again on the rocks. One of them stood on one of the blue tables lying on its side on the sand, staring at her with its beady eyes. She was used to the gulls always hanging around for food, but today they were oddly silent and she suddenly realised why. There was no sign of Socrates or his boat. When he was there, the gulls congregated around his boat, screeching and flapping, waiting for him to throw them the odd fish which sent them into a frenzy as they tried to steal the fish from each other. They always reminded her of hyenas after a kill. Often their screeching annoyed her, but today she missed them and their silence frightened her.

'Mama, what's wrong?' Georgia asked, seeing the look of concern on her face.

Nefeli was looking in the direction of the seashore where the tables and chairs lay strewn about.

'It's Socrates. He's not here.'

She realised she had been so caught up in worrying about the taverna that she'd completely forgotten about him.

'The storm was so bad maybe he put the boat away and went home. You said he knew it was coming,' Georgia said.

'Maybe,' Nefeli replied, but she felt a terrible sense of unease in the pit of her stomach.

Socrates was always there, mending his nets, even after a storm. He'd been a part of the landscape since she married and ran the taverna with Yianni. Something was dreadfully wrong. She told Georgia they should lock up the taverna for the time being and go to Chora to see what had happened to the rest of the islanders, but first she needed to see if her own boat and the arms her friends had stored away in the cave were still safe. She took the key from behind the basket on the wall and asked Georgia to collect the chairs and tables from the seashore while she went to check.

Even the cave had not been spared. The vicious waves had gushed over the rocks and poured into it from above, wedging the boat firmly against large rocks at the back. Thankfully it was undamaged. Most importantly the arms, which were stored between the rocks and almost a metre from the ground, were dry and safe, which was a great relief.

Back at the taverna, Georgia was busy collecting the tables and chairs from the beach, leaving them out to dry on the terrace along with the rest of the tables and chairs. Only one chair was damaged, but it was repairable. After leaving the windows open to air the place out, they headed to Chora.

Chapter 4

AGAMEMNON WAS SURE-FOOTED and cautious, and despite the mud and fallen rocks which blocked sections of the pathway, he wound his way slowly and safely up the hillside. Nefeli and Georgia heard the sound of church bells ringing through the hillside long before the village of Chora came into view. Nefeli was unsure of what she would find but the constant tolling was not a good sign. In the distance, perched on top of a hill, stood a cluster of whitewashed, flat-roofed houses with their brightly painted doors and windows. They spilled picturesquely down the hillside towards a cobalt-domed church with a magnificent view across the shimmering water towards Kalymnos and Kos. Other than for holy days — of which there were many — the bells rarely rang. At other times they rang because there was a death or a disaster. Nefeli remembered them clearly when the war started. It was said that they rang when the Turks left too, but that was a long time before she was born, although she did recall as a young child of five or six, that they tolled for the burning of Smyrna which the older islanders still talked about just as much as the current war. Now the sound was telling her they could only be tolling for a death.

Conscious of what the women had said to her about the men looking at her, she tucked strands of her stray black hair in her kerchief and covered her shoulders with her shawl before entering the village. The last thing she wanted to do was incur a vicious tongue lashing when the island was in such despair. As soon as they rounded the corner and entered the main street, incense wafted through the air and the peal of church bells was now joined by the haunting sounds of wailing and chanting coming from the square. That morning it seemed as if everyone on the island had gathered for what was evidently a solemn occasion. Nefeli ran her eyes over the throng of people to check who was there. Amid this scene of abject misery, Dimitri, standing at the back of the crowd, saw her and quickly pulled her aside and whispered in her ear about the events that had taken place during the night. They had attached limpet mines to a German naval vessel filled with troops destined for Rhodes and Crete, and blown it up.

She looked at him anxiously. 'Where are Michalis, Stratos and Pavlos? Did they survive?'

He shook his head. 'They didn't make it. We were in two separate boats when we made our getaway. I headed south with two men from Kalymnos, the others headed in a different direction but they were spotted by a patrol boat coming to the aid of the sinking ship. From a safe distance, we saw searchlights scanning the water and then heard gunfire. Minutes later there was another explosion and Michalis' boat sank. Luckily for us they didn't see us and we made it to back to land when the storm began.'

Nefeli felt the bile rise in her throat. '*Theé mou!*'

45

Dimitri apologised for being the bearer of such bad news. 'You just missed the Germans,' he continued in a low voice. 'They questioned everyone and have taken the mayor and schoolteacher away to Kos for interrogation.'

The shock of what took place during the night was quickly replaced by alarm. 'What on earth for? Don't tell me they were involved too?'

'I have no idea why they took them.' The way he dismissed the question made Nefeli think he was lying, but now was not the time to argue.

He pulled her away from the crowd a little more and at the same time urged her not to show any emotion or people would smell a rat. Nefeli felt her legs go weak at the knees and her throat was so dry she could barely speak. Georgia was watching her mother carefully. She knew her mother had received bad news but her pretty face hid the anxiousness she too felt. Life for the *andartes* since the Germans took over the islands was far more dangerous than anyone had expected. They would shoot first and ask questions later. Her island was tiny compared to others, but already they had lost at least fifteen men in the prime of their life — Yianni included.

'And Socrates?' Nefeli asked, scanning her eyes over the crowd. 'He isn't here either.'

Dimitri could barely look her in the eyes. 'He was out fishing when the storm hit. We saw him as we were leaving. Part of his caique was washed up on the rocks, but of Socrates...' It was hard for him to say the words. 'He has surely perished.'

'Oh God!' Nefeli covered her face with her hands. 'Are you sure it was his boat?'

'Only one caique on the island bears the name "Zephyr". There was no mistaking it.'

Nefeli felt a surge of anger. 'Why did he have to be out at night? So many times we warned him about the curfew.'

'He said you could catch certain fish only at night when it was a full moon. Last night was such a night.'

'I can't believe he would do such a silly thing. He knew there a bad storm brewing. He even warned me of it himself only the day before.'

Dimitri shrugged. 'Maybe he thought he'd get back before it hit. Socrates could be as stubborn as that mule of yours and he seemed to get worse with old age.'

Although he was speaking in a low voice, Georgia knew what they were saying. 'Mama, is Socrates dead?'

'Shhh!' Nefeli put her index finger to her mouth and told her not to say anything with people around. 'We don't know yet *agape mou*. We must pray for his safe return.'

On top of the devastation to the house and taverna, Nefeli was now forced to confront the fact that her closest friends were never coming back. No-one could have survived that storm. She thought of her last conversation with Michalis. He was the only person she felt she could she confide in. He had been a loyal and true friend and now he was gone. Her thoughts turned to the taverna. How would she survive without the fish Socrates gave her? It was a disaster.

Dimitri's wife, Toula, came over to join them. She had the two children with her, Stephanos, a boy the same age as Georgia, and a ten-month-old girl. She knew of her husband's activities with the *andartes* but never talked about it.

'Come,' she said to them, 'the priest is saying prayers. You can talk later.'

They solemnly joined the rest of the islanders. The prayers and chanting went on for an interminable amount of time. All knew it was a hopeless cause: they just wanted the bodies of the brave *palikaria* to wash up on the beach so they could be given a proper burial and not wander endlessly with the other lost souls in the underworld.

When the service was over, a few people gathered to socialise in the *kafeneia* around the square where a few drinks and *mezedes* were provided, courtesy of the owners due to the solemn occasion. People raised a glass to Socrates and spoke of him when he was young and Nefeli thought she would burst into tears at any moment.

Chora itself had survived the storm well with just a few battered shutters and broken plant-pots and containers. The fact that the houses were huddled together is what protected them.

'If the villagers don't know what took place, what do they think happened to the men?' Nefeli asked Dimitri.

'You know as much about these people as I do,' he replied. 'They suspected the men were *andartes,* but they won't say anything for fear of reprisals. They are putting on a brave face! They know a ship was blown up and must suspect their involvement in it. Let's leave it at that. As for Socrates — it was almost as if he had a death wish — going out to sea when he knew there would be a storm! Maybe he wanted to leave this world on his own terms; who knows?'

Nefeli couldn't believe that.

'Anyway,' Dimitri continued. 'How did you go with the storm? Was there any damage to the house and taverna?'

'The roof blew off the outhouse and parts of it fell down, and the chicken coop needs fixing. The animals are sharing the house with us. As for the taverna, that got a good soaking and the rush matting on the terrace needs repairing. All things considered, we were lucky.'

He offered to come and repair the damage for her. 'You can't keep those animals in the house for long, you know. They'll stink the place out.'

Knowing the villagers would gossip if a man came to the house alone, Toula offered to come with him to keep her company.

'Then there will be no wagging tongues,' she said with a wink.

Nefeli gladly accepted. Dimitri was a good carpenter so hopefully the repairs wouldn't take too long. The sombre mood continued and Nefeli decided to go back to the taverna. The floor would be dry by now.

'We'll call by the house tomorrow morning,' Dimitri said. 'Nice and early, so we can get the job done in a day.'

Nefeli had just lifted Georgia onto Agamemnon when she saw Kyria Eleni heading over.

'Have you thought any more about our conversation?' she asked.

'I have,' Nefeli replied.

'And...?'

'And you are right; it's been too long.' She glanced at Georgia. 'For the sake of my daughter, I think it's time I took another husband.'

Kyria Eleni clapped her hands together in delight. 'My dear, you are doing the right thing.'

In reality, Kyria Eleni relished the idea of being a successful matchmaker. It brought with it a lot of prestige and respect from the islanders, not only on their own tiny island, but as far away as Astypalaia, Kos and Kalymnos.

'On one condition,' Nefeli said.

'What's that?'

'He must be a good man and I must have some feeling for him.'

'Of course,' Kyria Eleni said, eager to agree. 'Yianni was a good man and I am sure he would be happy you've come to this decision.' She bid her farewell and said she would come to see her at the taverna.

The fact that she had mentioned her beloved Yianni made Nefeli despondent. No-one could ever replace him, but times were hard and there was no room for sentimentality. After almost four years of trying so hard to maintain her independence, she was now ending up like thousands of other Greek women — marrying not for love but because it was what was expected of them and there was no other way out.

When Kyria Eleni was out of earshot, Georgia shouted angrily at her mother. 'Mama, why did you say that — you have me? I don't want another daddy.'

Nefeli wasn't in the mood to argue. 'Shush! Please be a good girl. We'll discuss this later.'

'No, Mama,' Georgia cried out, the tears falling down her cheeks. 'You loved Papa. You told me no-one would ever take his place.'

Nefeli closed her ears to her daughter's pleas, but Georgia would not stop sobbing. Outwardly, Nefeli appeared cool and resolute: in reality, her heart was broken at the thought that she'd now committed herself to another marriage. She knew that before the crowd dispersed, they would all be aware of her agreement to take another husband. Kyria Eleni would make sure of that.

The sombre mood continued until they reached the taverna. The heat of the day had dried the floor nicely and Nefeli busied herself trying to tidy up the place. A few licks of paint here and there and the taverna would be like new. Only the roof over the terrace needed repairing but that was the last thing on her mind. Uppermost was how she would feed her few meagre customers without a regular supply of fish. There were so little vegetables in the garden and what there had been were ruined in the storm. She called Georgia to help her move the wet sacks of food. When there was no reply, Nefeli went outside to see where she was. She was sitting in the same spot where Socrates used to keep his boat, sobbing. Angrily, Nefeli stormed off towards her. She had too much to think about for such tantrums; what was done could not be undone and she couldn't afford to feel guilty about her actions. Georgia tried to run away but Nefeli caught her arm.

'Listen carefully, *Georgaki mou*. You cannot carry on like this. It breaks my heart to see you so unhappy, but you *must* understand this is for the best. You are a smart girl; surely you can see the dilemma we are in.'

'No,' Georgia answered defiantly. 'I can help you.'

'My darling, you are my soul and I love you very much, but you are still a child. You must study. One day soon this war will be over and I want you to make something of yourself — go away from here — Athens, America — have a better life. For that you must study hard. There's nothing for you here but hard work.' Nefeli hugged her tightly. Georgia breathed in her mother's scent– a mixture of fragrant orange blossom and chamomile, and it soothed her as it always had done since she was a baby.

'I loved your father and I will love him till the day I die, but life is just too hard. I need to have a man around. Please understand. Our life will be much easier.' She put her finger under her daughter's chin and looked into her eyes. 'You must trust me. I will only marry a good man and he will love you too. I will never bring anyone into our home who doesn't accept you as his own.'

Georgia saw her mother's eyes were glistening and realised she was making her life more difficult with her tantrum. She apologised. 'Alright, Mama; I want you to be happy.'

Nefeli wiped away the tears from Georgia's cheeks and then cradled her in her arms again, running her fingers through her silky long hair. 'We will always have each other, *agape mou*. That makes me happy.'

There was little more to be said. Nefeli had made up her mind, albeit reluctantly. The death of her friends, the destruction caused by the storm, looking after the taverna: it was all too much for her. She was exhausted. It was like a bad dream and she wanted nothing more than to curl up into a ball and sleep and wake up to a world without problems. That was impossible.

'Come on,' Nefeli said. 'Let's go home now. We've done everything we can here. The animals need feeding and we have to be up nice and early for Dimitri and Toula.'

Georgia slept soundly that night, but it was another sleepless one for Nefeli. She lit a candle to burn in the niche next to the icon of the Virgin and prayed for the souls of her friends. She tried so hard to be strong for Georgia, but without her friends, she felt alone. She opened the large painted wooden chest that contained much of her dowry — embroideries, kilims, fine silverware and a few pieces of porcelain and glassware — and pulled out an old tin decorated with images of Constantinople: the Hagia Sophia, bucolic scenes of fine waterside mansions and palaces, and caiques and ships sailing along the Bosporus. Inside were her most treasured possessions — a couple of photographs of Yianni and one he took of her sitting on a rock near the Blue Dolphin. She took out those of Yianni and studied them closely: the eyes that had looked at her so often: the mouth that had kissed every inch of her body: the way his black hair fell towards one side, especially when he danced. It was all she had left of him, but she didn't need a photograph to remind her of their love. That was embedded in her heart — and there was Georgia — the fruit of that love.

With tears in her eyes, she asked him if she was doing the right thing by taking another husband. She wanted a sign from him, but none was forthcoming. All he said that day when he left was that if he did not return, she must live her life as she thought right, both for herself and Georgia. He had provided her with a house and the Blue Dolphin taverna, but she must do whatever made her happy. He died before the Germans took Greece, never knowing the hardships they endured.

She put the photographs back in the tin. As a mother, Georgia was now uppermost in her mind. She wanted a better life for her. For that she was prepared to take another man.

Chapter 5

NEFELI AND GEORGIA were fast asleep when Dimitri and Toula arrived the next day with the two children. Nefeli looked at the time. It was seven o'clock. She jumped out of bed shaking Georgia and telling her to get dressed quickly. Georgia rolled over and yawned.

'We told you we would be early,' Dimitri said, unloading a sack of tools on the terrace while Toula tied up the mule and gave it a drink of water.

'I've had difficulty sleeping since the storm,' Nefeli replied.

Luckily Nefeli had washed the floor the night before and tethered the goats to an olive tree near the terrace door, but because the chickens were still inside, the place reeked of animals. Dimitri sniffed the foul air and went to inspect the chicken coop. It needed fewer repairs than the outhouse so he decided to start on that straightaway. He took his son with him. In the meantime, Nefeli prepared breakfast while Toula put her small daughter in Georgia's wooden rocking cradle. She sat on the divan next to it, rocking it to and fro with her foot to get the child back to sleep again.

'After you left Chora yesterday, I overheard Kyria Eleni telling Kyria Kalliope and Kyria Angeliki you had decided to take another husband. Is that right?'

Nefeli glanced over her shoulder to the other room where Georgia was dressing herself. She put a finger to her lips and told her to keep her voice down.

'Shhh! Yes, but Georgia is not happy about it.'

Toula said she thought she'd made a wise decision and that Georgia would soon warm to the idea. She stopped when Georgia came into the room, rubbing her eyes which were still red from crying.

'Come and give your Aunt Toula a hug,' Toula said, giving Georgia a loving cuddle. 'Are you being a good girl for your mother?'

Georgia nodded.

'She is always a good girl, aren't you?' Nefeli said, as she put the food on the table. 'Will you be a darling and go and tell Dimitri and Stephanos their breakfast is ready.'

Georgia, still yawning, did as she was told.

'Toula, please don't talk about this in front of her. She has to get used to the idea and at the moment she doesn't like it.'

Toula nodded. 'You don't have to worry. I wouldn't want to upset her. She's a good child. When do you expect to do something about...' Toula paused for a moment to find the right words, 'your situation?'

'I expect the women will come to the taverna in the next few days with a proposal. Rest assured, I shall consider the man in question carefully.'

'Yianni was a good man, Nefeli, and I'm sure he would agree you are doing the right thing.'

Georgia returned with Dimitri and Stephanos and they ate a hearty breakfast of olives, mulberry jam, almonds and walnuts, all from her garden. It was accompanied by small triangular pies made of *horta* and feta that Toula had prepared before they left. The pies were drizzled with thick honey which someone had kindly given Nefeli after she commented on its glorious fragrance of wildflowers and thyme which the beekeeper was fortunate to have in abundance near his hives. It was a simple and hearty meal that nourished both body and soul.

Dimitri said he'd already mended the chicken coop as it only needed the uprights hammering in place and the wire fencing securing. 'Now we'll start on the outhouse. If these two help me,' he glanced across at Stephanos and Georgia, 'then we'll have it finished today.'

As soon as breakfast was over, they went back to work, leaving Nefeli to clear the breakfast table and scrub the kitchen floor while Toula breast-fed her daughter. After she'd given the floor a good wash, she sprinkled orange flower water everywhere to perfume the house. Already the warm sun was coming through the open door and windows and soon the foul animal smells started to dissipate.

'I really should go and help Dimitri,' Nefeli said, 'but I'm so exhausted.'

Toula patted the divan and told her to sit down and relax. She put her daughter back in the cradle and took her embroidery out of a bag. Nefeli asked what she was working on.

'A cushion for my window seat; the old one's worn out through sitting on it for hours on end, staring out to sea in the hope that Dimitri returns safely.' She crossed herself at the memory of their lost friends. 'I could have easily lost him as well. I shudder to think what I would do without him.'

Toula showed Nefeli her embroidery. It was exquisite. Worked on white linen, it had two matching borders of flowing flowers and pomegranates with a single geometric house in the centre of each border flanked by tall cypress trees. The colours were mostly shades of red and indigo, except for the cypress trees which were green. Like most of the islanders, Toula dyed the colours herself. Only the green was purchased. Before the war, gypsy women used to visit the island a couple of times a year selling an array of yarns, fabrics and haberdashery such as buttons and ribbons. It was a while since they'd been and rumour had it that the Germans had sent them away — somewhere north out of Greece to a place they'd never heard of and found difficult to pronounce. These days, few people came to the island.

'I haven't embroidered for a while,' Nefeli said, but I do make cloth for Georgia and myself.' She showed Toula what she was weaving on the loom. 'It's for a skirt. I'm trying to introduce blocks of colour into the stripes for a decorative hem. The rest will be white.'

Toula commented on how fine it looked and they compared notes on dying as she had recently dyed a hank of yarn a beautiful shade of brown made from walnut shells. She resumed her seat and Nefeli sat at the loom and continued where she left off, deftly throwing the shuttle from one side to the other.

'Have you thought about selling the taverna?' Toula asked.

'Who would buy it? I would get nothing for it with a war on.

Besides, I haven't got the heart to sell something Yianni made for us.'

Toula changed the subject. 'Have you heard the Allies have landed in France?'

Nefeli realised she must have got this from Dimitri who got it from the *andartes* on one of the larger islands. Few people on the island had a radio and news was mostly passed by word of mouth.

'I have — but France is not Greece is it? It seems that after the debacle trying to free the Dodecanese Islands, the Allies are now putting all their efforts into freeing the rest of Europe first, so it will be a while before we see the back of the Germans here.'

Both women were quiet for a while, thinking of the friends they'd just lost at sea.

'At least I was able to survive when Socrates gave me fish every day,' Nefeli said. 'The taverna owes me nothing so I will try and keep it going until life returns to normal.'

'Dimitri will still see to it that you get a supply of fish every now and then,' Toula said, trying to reassure her friend that everything would work out well in the end.

'How many fishermen are left on the island now?' Nefeli asked with a sigh. 'Maybe three at the most.'

Toula laughed. 'These days anyone with a boat calls himself a fisherman. It's about all we've got left to sustain us. You've got one haven't you? Didn't Yianni have a caique named after the taverna?'

'He did, but I'm no fisherman.'

'Surely you learnt something about fishing from those years you spent talking with Socrates. And you used to go out with Yianni occasionally, didn't you?'

Nefeli laughed at the thought of her fishing. 'We'll see. I might give it a go. Desperate times call for desperate measures. To be honest, after so many people drowning, I'm afraid of the sea.'

Toula made a tutting sound. 'You only need to go a few metres out, throw a net over the side and you'll catch something — but of course, if you had a husband to take care of you, then that would be a different matter. You could sit and weave all day.'

'And get bored!'

'Bah! My dear, you need someone to spoil you like those ladies in those fine houses on the bigger islands. They do nothing all day except entertain: drinking tea and coffee and listening to music. You'd like that, wouldn't you?'

'I'm not quite sure I would,' Nefeli replied. 'Even someone with servants has to run around after them.'

Toula had a light-hearted and kind nature, and being so isolated, Nefeli missed other women like her in her life. She didn't see her as often as she'd like. At midday, the women went outside to check how the repairs were coming along. Dimitri had completely restored and secured the outhouse, although it would need a new roof which he promised to do another day. They had lunch on the terrace and then took a light nap for two hours before Dimitri continued his work, this time chopping up a few fallen trees and branches ready for firewood and stacking it up against the side of the house. Stephanos and Georgia busied themselves with cleaning up the vegetable patch and re-potting broken containers of basil and flowers. When they'd finished, no-one would have imagined there had been such a terrible storm — except for the void in their hearts over their lost friends.

By late afternoon, Dimitri had done as much as he could and

the family headed home. He promised to return to make a new roof in a few days' time. Georgia was thoroughly exhausted and curled up on the divan in the kitchen with the cat purring at her side while Nefeli put Agamemnon and the goats back in their new home. The evening was still warm and it was most unlikely there would be another storm so they would be fine without a roof. With Georgia fast asleep, she picked up her shawl and decided to take a long walk along the coast to clear her mind and think about her future, which looked far from rosy at this point.

The pathway meandered along the seashore skirting the many coves and secluded beaches. As a rule, she always headed left towards the taverna. Tonight, she turned right towards Aphrodite's Cove, a place she and Yianni used to go to often when they were first married. The pathway led to the southern tip of the island where there was a tiny whitewashed church with a cobalt blue domed roof — the church of the Panagia Thalassini. These days it was hardly ever used. The main reason for it being in such an isolated and pristine part of the island was because it had once served as a beacon for Christian pilgrims on their way to other more famous churches on the larger Aegean Islands like Tinos and Patmos. Yianni told her the islanders once considered it famous for its miraculous healing powers and went to pray for a blessing, but with a war on, the islanders preferred to pray at the larger church in Chora: it wasn't safe to venture to lonely spots for fear of coming across German patrol boats on the lookout for the *andartes*.

Nefeli's island was completely surrounded with rocky coves and inlets with pristine sandy shores, and she loved it. There was a time when Yianni suggested they might move to a larger island, but both agreed they would miss the beauty of their surroundings they'd now become used to: the island had cast its spell on them both. At a certain point the path veered down through a rocky opening towards the seashore. Aphrodite's Cove was her own little sanctuary, hidden away from the rest of the world. It was here she came when she needed to think. She took off her shoes and walked barefoot along the deep bronze sand, still warm from the heat of the day, and breathed in the salty sea air.

The sun was already dipping behind the horizon, bathing the world in liquid gold which quickly changed into hues of orange and tangerine. The more the sun slipped into the water, the more its reflection in the sea intensified and with the last orange rays before twilight, the warm reds soon turned into mauves. In a space of a few minutes, those mauves melted into inky blues and the night sky was awash with a thousand stars. Nefeli watched the moon rise, its smiling face beckoning the stars as if conducting a majestic orchestra. In a world filled with traumatic events, she took solace in nature's beauty.

She lifted her skirt and waded into the cool water feeling the wet sand squelch between her toes. The tide was barely a placid ripple, lapping gently over her bare feet like fine, delicate lacework. Socrates used to tell her the ocean was fickle — like a woman, he said. At the time she'd laughed at him, but he was right. After a while she turned to go back home before it got too dark and spotted what looked like the remains of a boat wedged between the grey rocks. She took a closer look and could see it was part of a lifeboat that must have smashed against the rocks during the storm. She scrambled over them to see if there was anything else around. There was nothing. The waves must have carried the rest of the boat back out to sea. As she was looking, she noticed something on the sand, partially hidden behind a large boulder near the edge of the cove. What she saw gave her such a fright she took a step back in shock, almost slipping off the rock. Was she imaging things? It looked like a boot! Warily she made her way down onto the sand to take a closer look and quickly discovered the boot was not merely an odd boot: it belonged to a man lying face down in the sand. She let out a gasp, covering her mouth with her hand in shock.

'Theé mou,' she muttered aloud. 'God preserve us!'

The man's body looked as though it had hit the rock with such tremendous force it lay like a crumbled rag doll. At first she thought he was dead but when she knelt down and checked his pulse, she realised he was still alive. She noticed he was wearing a wedding ring on his right hand. *Someone's husband: someone's son.* Whoever he was, he was hanging on to life by a thread and would probably be dead in a few hours. She turned him over but because of his badly bruised and swollen face, it was hard to tell how old he was. He was of medium height with light blonde hair caked in a mixture of sand and blood. She cast her eyes over his clothing and noticed an embroidered Luftwaffe eagle over his right breast pocket. This alone, together with the look of his clothes, as tattered as they were, and his blond hair, told her he was a German Luftwaffe pilot.

She stood up and stared down at him wondering what she should do. He was the enemy and she should leave him there to die, but her heart told her she couldn't live with herself if she did that. She bent down again to check his clothing further, wondering if he might have a gun on him. She was right. Inside the breast pocket of his jacket was a Mauser HSc. Carefully she slid it out and slipped it into her skirt pocket. In one of his other pockets, she found a wallet. It was still wet but she managed to prise it open a little. It was his ID — Martin Tristan Werner Heindorf. She couldn't read German but knew what the two insignias meant. The first was a red, white and black image with a gold eagle in the centre underneath which was written *X Fliegerkorps.* The second insignia was a small black and silver cross signifying the Luftwaffe. Nefeli had already heard of *X Fliegerkorps* — the 10th Air Corps — from Michalis and the other *andartes* as they had played an important role in defeating the Allies. The rest of the contents in the wallet were stuck together. She'd have to dry it out first before she could identify anything else. There was another thing he had on him and she found it in his trouser pocket — a dagger with a black handle and the same image of a swastika and eagle. Michalis told her these pilots were given them in case they parachuted out of the plane and needed to free themselves if they became tangled in a tree. This particular one had the knife with a blade contained in its handle which she assumed made it easier to open and close when the other hand was occupied.

Nefeli took his pulse again. He was definitely alive. This time she noticed he was wearing a beautiful watch. She took it off and examined that too. It was a pilot's navigational watch and had the word Luftwaffe written on it. That also went into her pocket. She sat back in the sand wondering what to do. She knew if she told any of the islanders — especially the men — they would shoot him without hesitation. She looked across at the wreckage of the boat. What was a pilot doing in a lifeboat? A myriad of thoughts raced through her mind. In the end she decided she would try to get him home. What she would do then, she had no idea, but she couldn't just leave him to die. She slipped on her sandals and ran back home. By the time she arrived at the house, it was dark but there was enough light from the full moon to see what she was doing. After hiding the man's belongings in a cloth under a couple of rocks and hay in the outhouse, she saddled up Agamemnon in readiness to return to the cove. She was just about to head back when she heard Georgia's voice on the terrace.

'Mama, what are you doing?' When she saw Agamemnon, she looked astonished. 'Where are you going at this hour?'

Nefeli could see there was no point in keeping this away from her daughter. She went over and crouched down, clasping her daughter's hand.

'*Glyko mou*, can you keep a secret?'

'Mama you're frightening me.' The fear showed in Georgia's dark eyes.

'There's a man on the beach. He's badly injured and I don't think he'll live, but I must do what I can to see if I can save him.'

Georgia's eyes widened. 'If the man is injured, why did you try to hide it from me? I will help you. Let me come with you.'

Nefeli smoothed her daughter's cheek with the back of her hand. 'It's not as simple as that. The man is German. If anyone finds out what I'm doing they will kill him — he's the enemy. They will probably kill me too for trying to save him.'

Georgia looked even more alarmed.

'I can't live with myself if I don't try to save him,' Nefeli said. 'I was brought up a good Christian Orthodox woman. I must respect everyone as a human being.'

'And if he lives, what then? Will you give him up to the *andartes* or the villagers to kill him? Or will his people come looking for him and kill us? You've seen how cruel they can be. They've just killed our friends.' Georgia clung to her mother. 'I'm scared.' The tears in her eyes glistened in the moonlight.

Nefeli knew what she was doing was dangerous. If the *andartes* found out, it was likely she would be in deep trouble.

'I know. I'm afraid myself,' Nefeli replied. 'That's why this has to be our little secret. It's just between you and me. I cannot try to save him unless you agree.'

Georgia was older than her years but she respected her mother and nodded her agreement. 'Wait a minute,' she said and ran back inside the house. When she returned she had with her the icon of the Virgin. 'Let us pray to her to keep us safe.'

Together they closed their eyes, said a little payer and, when Georgia was satisfied the Virgin had heard their prayers, she took the icon back inside, gave her one more kiss for luck and placed it back on the shelf while Nefeli waited with Agamemnon.

'Fine,' Georgia said. 'We are safe now.'

Nefeli smiled. There were many times over the past four years, they'd prayed to the Virgin to look after them and she had always come through for them when they needed her most.

'Let's go,' she said, sitting Georgia on Agamemnon's back. 'There's no time to waste.'

Chapter 6

SOMETIME AROUND MIDNIGHT, Nefeli and Georgia arrived back at the house with the man. He was still unconscious and even weaker than before. It had not been easy to move him, but in the end they'd managed to slide him over Agamemnon's back by coaxing the animal to lie down next to him. They had no idea as to the extent of his injuries and in her heart, Nefeli thought he would not survive the night.

'What are we going to do with the boat?' Georgia asked. 'What if someone comes by and spots it. They'll search the island.'

There was little remaining of the boat and for the time being, they decided to drag it behind the rocks and cover it with clumps of grass and scrub and the odd piece of driftwood that had washed up beside it. Nefeli said she would return the next day and chop it up for firewood for the oven. Back at the house they carefully slid the man off Agamemnon's back and dragged him inside, laying him on a large kilim between the divan and the weaving loom. Nefeli lit the lantern and sent Georgia to settle Agamemnon in the outhouse for the night while she made sure the shutters were tightly closed.

'Bolt the door,' she said when Georgia returned. 'We don't want any unexpected visitors nosing around.'

Georgia doubted anyone would call in the middle of the night but did as she was told. The only people who had ever called late at night were Michalis, Stratos, Pavlos, and Dimitri and the first three were no longer alive. Nefeli sat on the divan wringing her hands. It was evident her mother was scared and had no idea what she was going to do with the man.

'Let's see if he lives through the night,' Nefeli said. 'If he's dead by morning, we'll bury him.' She told Georgia to try and get some sleep. It would all work out somehow.

Georgia disappeared through the alcove, slipped on her nightdress and nervously settled herself between the sheets.

'Don't be long, Mama. You need sleep too.'

When she was sure Georgia was fast asleep, Nefeli poured cool water into a basin, added a few dried herbs, and took it over to the man. She sat cross-legged on the kilim next to him, lifted his head onto a towel, and attempted to clean the sand and blood from his face with a soft sponge. It took three bowlfuls of water to clean him. Under the muck and grime the swellings and cuts looked terrible and it was impossible to tell if he had any broken bones or even if he could see, as his eyelids were too swollen to open. With the tips of her fingers, she gently prised his lips open and squeezed fresh water from a clean sponge into his mouth. The water dribbled out of the side of his mouth. She persisted for a few minutes longer, moving his head slightly to one side in order not to choke him. He had a perfect set of beautiful white teeth. Whatever force had swept him onto the rocks had not damaged any of them.

Her caring attempt at trying to clean his face had not roused him in the slightest. He was immune to her gentle touch — but she was not immune to him. It dawned on her that this was the first time she had touched another man's face since her husband. Four years was a long time. Realising her act of kindness had stirred dormant thoughts, she quickly pulled away and emptied the bowl. It was time to go to bed.

The next morning the German was still alive. Georgia could see her mother had attempted to clean his face but said nothing. Nefeli prepared her daughter's breakfast and together they ate in silence, staring at the stranger on the floor with mounting anxiety. Nefeli said it was too dangerous to leave him where he was and that they must hide him — but where? Outside was impossible as Dimitri would be back at any moment to finish the outhouse roof. Georgia suggested the cave where the Blue Dolphin caique was kept but Nefeli quickly ruled that out as the *andartes* stored weapons there. In the end, she suggested they move him into the room where they slept. Although it was only a small room separated by the alcove, no visitor ever went in there: it was a private space with the marital bed and the dowry chest. The problem was, the alcove was big enough for someone to see through and she suggested they cover the opening with a piece of fabric or another kilim. That way the man could lie on the floor out of sight.

She went to her dowry chest and pulled out fabrics and rugs she'd never used before. Many were woven by her mother, the others she'd woven for herself or Georgia's dowry. One by one they put aside those they considered large enough to cover the opening. There weren't too many that big. Some were too long and narrow, others were wide but not long enough. Others were simply too beautiful to use as a door covering, especial the ones with the gold embroidery. In the end they decided on a pair of identical matching kilims. Each one was almost floor to ceiling in length and when hung side by side would cover the opening well.

'Your *yiayia* wove these,' Nefeli said to Georgia. 'She was an accomplished weaver and made extra money by selling her textiles. She once told me a few people had offered to buy these two but they were not for sale; they were for me. I remember your other *yiayia* — Papa's mother — being impressed by them. It was one reason she wanted your father to marry me. "This woman will make you a good home," she told him.'

Nefeli rolled them out to check the length and width.

'They are certainly beautiful,' Georgia remarked, 'but aren't they too good to use as a room divider? Why not save them and use something simple instead?' She pointed to a pair of coarse multicoloured stripes which Nefeli had woven herself the year before with left over yarn.

Nefeli thought them far too plain and decided on the kilims. 'I think it's time to put these to good use and we can admire them at the same time. Now, I need you to help me hang them.'

They fetched the ladder from outside, careful to bolt the door again when they returned, and Nefeli set about hammering the upper hem of each carpet in place over the top of the alcove while Georgia held the weight of the carpet to make it easier.

'It's not good to do it this way,' Nefeli said, hammering the first one in place. 'They should be fixed properly — on a rod, but I don't have one. Next time we go to Chora, I will buy one.'

When the carpets were in place, Nefeli hammered a hook into

either side of the alcove wall and strung two long woven braids through them to tie the carpets back when needed. Both carpets had broad stripes across the width with a design consisting of alternating motifs of lozenges, diamonds, and bands of zig-zags. The colours were red, navy and cream with the occasional brown and the design of each one met in the centre of the alcove creating a beautiful composition. Most importantly, the carpets reached the ground so no one would be able to see the stranger behind them.

She stood back to admire her handiwork. 'There, now we can hide him and no-one will be any the wiser.'

Together they dragged the kilim with the German still lying on it, into the alcove. With the carpets hanging across the alcove, it was quite dark even though there was a small window at the side of the marital bed.

'I'm scared,' Georgia said. 'He could wake up and murder us!'

'Somehow I doubt that.' Nefeli laughed. 'The important thing is, no-one must know we are hiding him.'

Georgia was exasperated. 'You go to the taverna every day. You don't know how many times the Germans come to Chora and threaten us with death if we are caught hiding people.'

'*Andartes*, yes, but they are hardly going to shoot us for saving one of their own.'

Georgia frowned. 'No! But the villagers will. Look what happened to Pandelis and his wife. They were killed for being friendly to the Germans — by our own men!'

'No my darling; they were killed for collaborating. That's different.'

The story of how Pandelis and his wife died still reverberated through the island. A German patrol boat had dropped anchor near a deserted cove and Pandelis was spotted by a goatherd talking to them. The next day, the Germans raided Chora and Mikrolimano and took two men away accusing them of being *andartes*. The men were taken to another island and executed. When the news circulated about Pandelis having been seen with the Germans, a group of men paid him a visit late one night and questioned him. He denied having spoken with any German but when confronted with the goatherd's account, clearly became agitated. The men searched the house and soon discovered a wad of money in a tin under the bed. His futile attempts at explaining the money fell on deaf ears and both he and his wife were shot and their bodies dumped unceremoniously in the square. They stayed there for two days, decomposing in the heat because no-one dared to go near them. In the end, it was the Germans who moved the bodies during another surprise visit. They were thrown into the back of a truck and taken to Mikrolimano. There, they were unloaded off the truck and simply thrown into the sea. The islanders watched on in silence as the bodies bobbed up and down on the waves. After a few minutes, they sank, joining those before them on their final journey into the underworld. No-one mentioned them again and they were not mourned. Their house was burnt down by the villagers as a reminder to anyone else who might be thinking of betraying them.

All this made Georgia even more anxious. In her mind, being near any German was dangerous. 'Tell me, Mama, what do you intend to do if he lives?'

Nefeli had mulled over this problem in her head all night. 'It's possible I will use him as a bargaining tool. In exchange for us saving his life, we will get him to save the lives of any *andartes* locked up in Rhodes, Samos, Kos, or any of the other islands where they are held awaiting trial.'

At that moment there was a knock on the door and a woman's voice called out. 'Nefeli, are you there?'

It was Toula. She shouted again. Nefeli hastily pulled the kilims together and, after checking the German was well-hidden, opened the door.

'Is everything alright?' Toula asked. 'It's ten o'clock and you still have the shutters closed.' Nefeli opened them, saying they slept in. She asked Georgia to go and feed the animals.

'Aren't you going to school today, young lady?' Toula asked Georgia as she brushed past her.

'She isn't feeling too well,' Nefeli replied. 'The incident with the Germans in Chora scared her so I thought I'd keep her here with me for a few days. Anyway, they took the teacher to Kos, so what's the point.'

Toula put a basket of fish on the table. 'Another fisherman came round this morning and dropped it off. We thought that with Socrates gone, you might like some.'

Nefeli took a look. There was enough fish to last a few days if they were careful, and an octopus. She was grateful for anything she could lay her hands on.

'There's something else,' Toula added. 'Dimitri received word this morning that a German boat — possibly the one that spotted Michalis, Stratos and Pavlos — was lost in the storm. There's no sign of the main boat, but apparently there were two lifeboats and neither has been found. He thinks the Germans will be scouring the place again in case there are any survivors.'

Nefeli felt her throat tighten. 'Who could survive that storm? Besides, wouldn't they be closer to Kos? Why would they look here?'

Toula shrugged. 'Maybe it's just another excuse for a search.'

'If a large boat can't weather a storm, I'm sure a lifeboat can't either.' Nefeli's reply was sharp. She was worried. 'Why didn't we hear of this before?'

Toula put a hand on Nefeli's arm. 'Is everything alright?'

'Of course. I'm just on edge, that's all. The loss of our friends, the storm wreaking so much havoc, the mayor and the schoolteacher being taken away, and now we have to look forward to more searches. I try to stay strong for Georgia, but...' Nefeli sat on the window seat looking out at sea, 'it's all beginning to get me down. When will it end?'

'We're all in this together, my friend. Try and snap out of it and get this fish filleted before it goes off. It's going to be another scorcher of a day. I've got a supply that's already been salted. You should do the same.' Toula emptied the basket. As she did so, she sniffed the air. 'There's a smell of dampness in here. Are you sure you didn't get a leak during the storm?'

Nefeli realised straight away it was the damp clothes the soldier was still wearing and the sodden kilim he was lying on. Toula was right. The place smelt of damp wool and she'd been too busy to notice.

'I'd forgotten I had a sack of wool outside waiting to be spun and it got wet in the storm.'

Toula cast her eyes around the room. They rested on the kilims hanging across the alcove. 'They weren't there the last time I was here.' She walked towards them and brushed her hand across them. Nefeli stood rooted to the ground, holding her breath praying she wouldn't look behind them.

'I decided to cheer the place up a little and hung them up yesterday. They were part of my dowry. My mother made them for me. It's a pity to keep them locked away in the chest.'

Toula's finger traced a section of the pattern. The kilim was quite heavy and barely moved. 'Exquisite. I recall she was an excellent weaver.'

Thankfully, Toula already knew the marital bed and dowry chest were on the other side of the alcove and the kilims only served to state that it was Nefeli's private space. Toula would respect that fact. Nevertheless, if the kilims parted just a little, then it was possible she would see the German lying there. Nefeli's heart pounded in her chest at the thought of it.

'Beautiful,' Toula repeated, full of admiration. She turned and picked up the basket. 'Now I'd best get on home. I'll try and come back when Dimitri returns to fix the roof on the outhouse. It could be in a couple of days. He mentioned he might have to go to one of the other islands to pick up some things.'

Relieved to see Toula move away from the alcove, Nefeli breathed a sigh of relief and thanked her once more for the fish, promising to return the favour. When she'd gone, Nefeli slumped on the divan.

'That damp smell almost gave us away,' she said to Georgia.

'What are you going to do? We can't exactly put him outside to dry can we?'

'I'll have to take his clothes off. We'll find a place to dry them: somewhere from prying eyes.'

She asked Georgia to stay outside while she did it. 'Go and

finish tidying up. I'm sure there are some things you can find to do after the storm.' She looked at the fish on the table, gathered it up in newspaper and handed them to her. 'You can start by salting these and hanging them out in the sun to dry. Don't forget to clean them well first and rub them with plenty of salt. We will eat the octopus tonight.'

Chapter 7

NEFELI CAREFULLY UNBUTTONED the man's jacket and opened it wide, exposing the shirt underneath. Turning him to one side, she gently pulled off the first jacket sleeve and then the other. There was nothing else in any of the pockets. Next was the shirt. The buttons were much smaller and she was forced to kneel closer, her face so close to his that it sent shivers down her spine. As she undid each button, her eyes kept darting to his face; afraid he might wake up at any moment and catch her. The shirt was tucked into his trousers and to free it, she had to remove his leather belt and open the top of his trousers. That too, had a button. With each undone button, she felt a strange stirring in her body. The shirt came off easily. Underneath, he wore an off-white cotton vest which she noted was of excellent quality. She moved his arms and pulled it over his head and then stopped for a moment, leaning her back against the dowry chest surveying his unscathed torso. There was hardly a mark or a cut on it, just a few honey-coloured blemishes which she surmised might be old combat bruises from an earlier encounter of some sort. Only his face showed signs of bruising and swelling and they weren't as bad as she first thought. It was as if he was sleeping. Now she had to remove the trousers. That was going to be the hardest part. Before she could do that, she took off his heavy boots. They were easier to remove than she'd imagined. Next were the socks. The stench of dampness filled the air even more and she quickly picked everything up and took it outside. Georgia was not far away, collecting broken wood and putting it in a heap near the oven. She called her over.

'Take these and lay them out in the sun. We'll burn them when they are dry.' Georgia screwed up her face at the smell. 'Don't be long; I still need you to keep watch in case anyone pays us a visit.'

Nefeli returned to the house, careful to close the door behind her. Outside, the sun was beating down and she opened the windows and shutters to let in the light and warmth. A shaft of light highlighted the man's torso — fit and muscular — like the body of Christ in a religious scene. She crossed herself and said a little prayer asking God and the Virgin to forgive her for what she was about to do. Then she set about removing his trousers which were tight and stuck to his body like a second skin. There was no other option but to cut them off. She fetched her scissors from the loom and, inch by inch, cut them away, a leg at a time. Each time a piece of fabric came away she saw the beauty of his shape. It was like unearthing an ancient statue, except that this wasn't marble or stone rendered smooth by a sculptor: here was a man — a living, breathing body created by the finest sculptor of all — God himself. When she reached his groin, she stopped. Her hands were trembling. Not only was she afraid she might accidentally hurt him, she thought it would make her a sinner in the eyes of God.

She glanced at the photograph of Yianni hanging over the marital bed next to the icon of the Virgin and felt a tinge of betrayal but reasoned that what she was doing was helping another human being. She wondered if someone — another caring woman — might have tried to save him too. She still wasn't sure exactly how he died but it warmed her heart to think his last memories were of kindness. *Forgive me darling for what I am doing.*

It wasn't the thought of Yianni that bothered her so much, but the Virgin Mary, staring down at her from the ornate, silver frame. Then she remembered it was the women who washed Christ when he was taken from the cross. Mary Magdalene too — the woman some called a prostitute. Even then, people thought the worst. If the villagers on the island knew what she was doing now, she too would be labelled a prostitute. Nothing had changed. All the same, she turned the icon to face the wall before continuing.

Slowly and gently, with one hand, she slipped her fingers beneath the last cut at the man's trousers and with the other hand, pushed the tip of the scissors under the cloth and carefully snipped away, using the tiniest of cuts. She was becoming used to his body now, taut and covered with the finest of blonde hair, but when she felt a different kind of hair, she let out a gasp. *God give me strength.* She got up and went outside to check where Georgia was. She was nowhere in sight but she could see the goats in the distance and knew she wasn't too far away.

She returned to the man and continued. Within a few minutes, the rest of his trousers fell away along with his underwear. When she saw his genitalia, she quickly covered her mouth with her hand. His phallus was lying to one side, nestling on his scrotum and partially covered by his pubic hair which glistened in the sunlight. She couldn't stop staring. He was like a Greek God — just like the images she'd seen in books at school: Zeus, Poseidon, and all the others — beautiful and perfect. She'd never thought about it before, but it occurred to her that they were never ashamed of their nakedness and manliness. It also occurred to her that she'd never thought of Yianni as a Greek God either, even though he'd had a good physique.

Nefeli recalled the first time she'd seen Yianni's phallus. She was young and innocent, and it frightened her until Yianni's sweet words told her it was nothing to be afraid of. He had names for it too, like "little bird" or the "snake". It made her laugh. He also had other names which he said were too rude to tell her. She soon learnt to love his "little bird" because she loved him deeply. It was he who taught her that private parts were nothing to be ashamed of: something beautiful to be admired — between lovers only.

The stranger's physique was different. Yianni was smaller and much darker-skinned. This man was tall, his pale Northern European skin bronzed from the Mediterranean sun. Her eyes lingered on his phallus a few moments longer and her heightened emotions caused her to bite her lip. She slowly began to trace the contours of his muscles from his collarbone and across his chest with her index finger. He was ravishing. At the same time, Nefeli realised how long it was since she'd been ravished. All of a sudden, she felt a strong urge to kiss his fingertips. They tasted salty. The urge satisfied, she rested his hand by his side again, fetched some clean water and sponged his body. Rather than think of him as the enemy, she imagined herself washing the body of Christ. Finally, she covered him with a clean blanket.

Nefeli picked up the cut pieces of fabric, stuffed them in an old wool sack, and put them outside to burn later that night with the rest of his clothes. The damp kilim was laid out over the nearby rocks to dry. Then she set about sorting through Yianni's old clothes and pulled out a white cotton shirt and a pair of trousers. Maybe the trousers were too short, but then maybe — just maybe — the stranger might not pull through.

When Georgia returned, the stranger lay behind the closed kilims on another clean kilim. She noted that the damp smell had been replaced with a fragrant herbal scent — chamomile, mountain herbs, and orange blossom. Her mother always kept bunches of various herbs hanging from hooks underneath a shelf, and on top, were an assortment of small boxes, bottles and jars containing orange blossom and rose water, dried peels, saffron, and mastic tears. Georgia's observant eyes noted that some had been used and pounded down with the pestle and mortar which stood in the sink.

'He's still alive then?' she asked with a hint of disdain.

'It's touch and go: his pulse is still low. There are no physical marks on his body, only the bruised face, but we can't be sure if there was internal or brain damage when he was swept ashore.'

Georgia poked her head behind the kilims to take a look. To her it seemed as if he was sleeping peacefully on the floor.

'What are we going to do now?' she asked, uncomfortably. 'We can't sleep in there with him.'

'Of course not,' Nefeli replied. 'We can sleep in here on the divan. It's much smaller but if it's too cramped I will make a bed for myself on the floor next to you.'

After supper Nefeli hid the boots with his other belongings in the outhouse and they lit a fire and burnt all his clothes. They watched them burn and talked about what they would do if he didn't die. Georgia, who had now taken to calling the stranger "the invisible man", fervently hoped he would die. Her mother wasn't so sure.

Chapter 8

THERE WERE QUITE a few people out and about in Chora when Nefeli arrived. Some of the old men sat outside the *kafeneia* playing *tavli* and cards, trying their best to carry on as if life was normal. The priest was also with them. It took their minds off the war and their sons and grandsons who had left the village at the start of the war or joined the *andartes*. She tied Agamemnon to a tree outside a whitewashed house with turquoise blue shutters and knocked on the door. A small woman dressed in black and wearing a crocheted shawl opened the door.

'Kyria Nefeli,' Kyria Eleni said, giving her a welcoming smile. 'I am so glad to see you. Come in.'

Kyria Eleni's two-roomed house was even smaller than Nefeli's, but it was comfortable and extremely tidy, even though there were far too many things adorning the walls for Nefeli's liking. In fact, they were completely covered, making the rooms even smaller. The old photographs Nefeli could understand, even the six icons and a few embroideries, but there were also faded paintings of Greek temples and bucolic scenes which should have been thrown away years ago.

Kyria Eleni moved a large tray of dried beans from the table and set a copper briki of coffee on the stove. Except for the rhythmic stirring of the spoon in the briki and the occasional chirping of Kyria Eleni's canary hanging in a wooden cage outside the window sill, the place was silent, cocooned by other whitewashed houses that nestled around it. Nefeli had been brought up in such a house and when she moved to the house that Yianni built near the sea, she relished the space and freedom it brought with it. There, she could hear the wind whistle through the olive trees and their fruit orchard, listen to the waves, and taste the salty sea air when a wind whipped up the sea at night.

'Now, my dear,' Kyria Eleni said, as she spooned the *kaimaki* into the small cups and then poured the rest of the coffee in. 'I am presuming this visit is about our conversation the other day?'

'Yes. As I said, I've given it some thought and decided I should consider taking another husband after all.'

Kyria Eleni gave her a toothless smile. 'A wise decision, but if you don't mind me asking, what made you decide? I mean, you didn't seem at all receptive to the idea when we were there. In fact, Kyria Angeliki and Kyria Kalliope got the distinct feeling you couldn't wait to see the back of us.'

Nefeli shifted uncomfortably in her chair. 'It wasn't that I didn't appreciate your concern: it's just that I am happy alone. I have Georgia and the taverna and that's more than enough to keep me occupied. And as you know, I loved my husband very much.'

'I know my dear, but a woman needs a man around the place.' Kyria Eleni winked. 'Especially if they are young and beautiful as you are.' She took a sip of her coffee. '*Every heart sings a song, incomplete until another heart whispers back. Those who wish to sing always find a song.'*

'*At the touch of a lover, everyone becomes a poet.* Plato isn't it?' Nefeli replied.

Kyria Eleni laughed. 'We were taught that at school.'

Nefeli smiled. Kyria Eleni could barely write her own name and it surprised her to think she could quote someone like Plato.

'It may surprise you to know that I married twice,' Kyria Eleni said. 'Just like you, I lost my first husband soon after we were married — the Great War. Then I married his brother. He looked after me well until he died, fifteen years ago.'

'I had no idea,' Nefeli replied. 'Tell me, did you love him as much as you did your first husband?'

'My dear, what sort of question is that? It was arranged – *proxenio* — by my parents. I was only seventeen when the first one died and I barely knew him. It was our families who decided I should marry his brother. He was a good man; kind and thoughtful, but we were not fortunate enough to be blessed with a child. That was our only curse. As for "love" — I am not sure what you really call love. We respected each other and cared for one another. He was a good provider and I was a good wife, so we were happy. What more can you ask?'

It didn't sound at all romantic to Nefeli, who wanted more from a marriage than that.

'Besides, a woman who doesn't have a man in her bed soon becomes a wizened old crone when her looks fade.' She indicated to a jar of dried black olives on the sideboard, leaving Nefeli in no doubt as to the exact meaning of her statement.

Nefeli took a deep breath. 'I have decided to take another

man because of Georgia. I was managing to get by at the taverna because of the fish Socrates used to give me daily along with the few vegetables and fruit I grow, but now it is difficult. We will starve if we continue this way. I am thinking of her, not me.'

'Have you discussed it with her?'

'Yes. It's rather a delicate situation and she is not happy about it. She doesn't know I am here with you, so please don't say anything. I will tell her when the time is right.'

There was an awkward silence for a few minutes while the two finished their coffee.

It was Nefeli who spoke first. 'Did you have anyone in mind? There are so few unmarried men of marriageable age on the island and most have left to join the *andartes*.'

'If you give me a day or two, I will consult with Kyria Angeliki and Kyria Kalliope. We will put our heads together and come up with a very nice man.' Kyria Eleni reached across the table and patted Nefeli's hand. Her fingers were old and bony; a sharp contrast to Nefeli's soft hand with her slender fingers and beautifully shaped nails. 'Don't worry, my dear, we have your best interests at heart.'

Kyria Eleni saw her to the door. 'Would you like us to come and see you at the house?'

Nefeli turned swiftly. 'No. Please don't!' She realised she'd said it much too quickly and attempted to qualify her words. 'I won't be there. I must return to the taverna. Hopefully a few more customers will drop by. Come around lunchtime and I will prepare us something to eat.'

'That is very kind of you, but we don't want you to go to any trouble.'

'It's the least I can do to repay your kindness,' Nefeli said.

'Perhaps we should make a time now. What about Friday. Does that suit?'

'That gives us three days, but it should be fine.'

'Excellent. I will expect you around midday.'

Nefeli unhooked Agamemnon's rope and walked away towards the square. There were a few things she needed to get before the shops closed for the afternoon siesta. She entered Konstantinos Vervatis' store to get a curtain rod. Above the entrance was a large blue wooden sign which bore the name, *O Ermis*, after the God Hermes. Underneath was written the word, *Pantopoleion*, in large black and white letters painted with a naïve flourish. The store was more a bric-a-brac store than a general grocery as it sold everything from copper pots, agricultural implements such as scythes, birdcages, tables and rush-bottomed chairs, haberdashery, to wine and spirits in barrels or bottles. The sign had been painted by the same itinerant painter Yianni hired to decorate his house and bore his name in the corner. Inside, there was very little space to manoeuvre as the place was crammed from floor to ceiling with products, some of which Nefeli was sure had been there for years. Towards the back of the room, the owner kept a wooden table and a few chairs for his friends who occasionally stopped by for a drink and a chat. A group of people were gathered there playing cards over drinks. When Konstantinos saw her, he excused himself from his card game to serve her.

'Good day, Kyria Nefeli. What can I do for you?'

He gave her a beaming smile. Konstantinos had always had a soft spot for Nefeli since she was a small girl and it had always been his intention to marry her — until Cassandra came along.

Cassandra wasn't as attractive as Nefeli, but her prospects were much more advantageous as her parents had money. She had been a good wife until she died in childbirth. Without a wife and children to help, Konstantinos was burdened to look after the store and keep house alone.

'I'd like a curtain rod,' Nefeli replied. She gave him the measurements and he pulled three styles out from behind a pile of chairs. She chose the simplest and the cheapest: a wooden one with detachable ball-shaped ends. 'And two hooks to sit them on.'

'Is there anything else?'

'A bottle of raki, please.' Nefeli noticed the men had stopped talking and were staring at her. 'Is everything alright?' she asked, in a low voice.

'We were discussing the recent events.'

Nefeli felt an overwhelming guilt, as if the whole island had eyes and knew her secret. 'Which events would they be?'

'The fact that the mayor and the schoolteacher are still locked up on Kos. There is talk that they will be either executed or deported.'

'What for: they haven't done anything wrong, have they?' Nefeli suspected they might have aided the *andartes* in their capacity as minor bureaucrats, but as far as she knew, that was as far as it went. They were careful never to carry guns, and she was sure *andartes* such as Michalis, Pavlos, Stratos and Dimitri would tell them as little about their work as possible in order not to endanger their lives. It was one of their rules.

'They say that during the storm, a German boat was lost. It had two lifeboats. They found one washed up on Astypalaia. Three

Germans managed to save themselves but they have no idea what happened to the second and are out searching the islands. They're threatening to take hostages if any of the villagers have killed them.'

Nefeli felt a shiver run down her spine.

Konstantinos took a bottle of raki from a shelf and put it in a brown bag.' He leaned forward and whispered. 'It's a good one — smuggled in from Turkey.' He gave her a cheeky wink. 'This one's made from raisins. It will go well with fish.'

Nefeli took some money out of her purse to pay him, but he put his hand out to stop her. 'Put it back. I know things are tough these days. Dimitri told us the house suffered in the storm, and with Socrates gone, we know things can't be easy for you. You can cook us a nice meal one day in return.'

He then took a few boiled sweets out of a jar and wrapped them in a piece of paper saying they were for "the little one". She thanked him. It seemed the whole island knew she was having a hard time.

'Take care,' he shouted after her. 'Just in case the Germans start searching the island: they are not always kind to our women.'

Nefeli put the raki in the pannier, tied the curtain rod on Agamemnon's back and started back down the hill. Within ten minutes, the village of Chora, nestling between the hilltops, was out of sight. The path meandered through the sweet-smelling scrubland towards the coast with a beautiful view of Kalymnos and Kos in the distance. Mountain ranges merged into a haze against the clear blue sky, almost floating in the shimmering heat. At one point, she sat on a rock to survey the beauty surrounding her. There was not a breath of wind; only the searing hot sun which was impossible to escape. She ran her hands through her hair and in an attempt to get some air, pulled her blouse away from her shoulders and lifted up her skirt, exposing her thighs. Her olive skin was moist with sweat. She undid the ties at the front of her blouse and shook it several times with the tips of her finger. The curves of her firm breasts glistened. She closed her eyes and ran her hand over them, remembering the times Yianni had caressed them. How she missed his touch. In just a matter of a couple of days, she'd become aware of her body again. It was the main reason she had gone to see Kyria Eleni. Not because she needed another man to feed herself and her child; she could scrape through as others did and the war wasn't going to last forever. Besides, she had her orchard, vegetable garden, the Blue Dolphin and the boat. If need be, she could sell the last two. That would give her money to tide her over. Maybe she could even work for the new owner. No, it wasn't really the money, it was that she realised she was still a young woman in the prime of her life. That's what the stranger had done to her. How could someone, barely clinging to life as he was, have such a profound effect? This strange sense of being that had taken hold of her was confusing.

She continued on her way until she came to a fork in the pathway. She had intended to take the path on the right which led to the house but something caught her eye and she quickly changed her mind. A German patrol boat had dropped anchor in shallow waters near the Blue Dolphin and several men were searching the coastline. She tugged on Agamemnon's rein and set off towards them, arriving just as one of them was about to break open the taverna door.

'Stop!' she cried out. 'Your people came here the other day and searched the place. There's nothing for you!'

All around her she could see armed German soldiers combing the rocks.

The soldier about to break open the door pointed a rifle and bellowed at her in German.

'I'm sorry. I don't understand,' Nefeli replied.

The German called a man over. Like the last Greek who had accompanied the previous Germans, he was not in uniform and Nefeli could not tell if he was a willing collaborator or someone forced to translate for them. A conversation ensued in German.

'Herr Oberleutnant Becker asks if this place belongs to you,' the Greek said.

'Yes, but I told him, there's nothing here. The taverna has been closed a few days now and they searched it before.'

The Greek didn't bother translating. 'Herr Oberleutnant Becker wants you to open up immediately.'

Nefeli looked exasperated. 'Tell Herr Oberleutnant Becker they searched the place a few days ago,' she repeated, sarcastically.

The Greek man, who appeared to be in his mid-thirties, told her not to provoke them and to do as they asked. He added that they were in a foul mood. Nefeli gave the man pointing the rifle at her a disdainful look and reluctantly did as she was told. Herr Becker beckoned to another two soldiers to search the place thoroughly. This time they were much rougher than before, pulling sacks open and spilling the contents on the floor, going through cupboards and drawers tipping their contents alongside the dried pulses and rice.

Nefeli begged the Greek to make them stop. He shrugged his shoulders but his eyes told her he was embarrassed at their behaviour. Herr Becker fixed his gaze on her while tapping his free hand on his thigh, impatiently. Someone outside called out his name and he went outside, telling the men to keep searching. Nefeli watched him through the window talking to another soldier.

'What's going on?' she asked the Greek.

'They are looking for two of their own who were caught in the storm — and also for weapons. It was a daring feat by the *andartes* to blow up the ship the other evening and they fear more will be targeted.'

Herr Becker stormed back with the second man. His face was red with anger. He barked something in German at the Greek

'They've found a boat in a cave bearing the same name as this taverna. They say the gate to the entrance is locked and Herr Oberleutnant Becker wants the key.'

Herr Becker put his face so close to Nefeli's she could smell his breath. *'Sofort– und keine Spiele spielen,'* he shouted, angrily.

The Greek told her he said she wasn't to play games. It was in her interest to give them the key now.

Nefeli hesitated. 'And what if I don't?' she asked defiantly.

The Greek looked nervous and reiterated again it was in her best interest to comply. 'I have seen what they do to our women. I beg you, if you don't have anything to hide, be courteous.'

'Courteous! Tell him that was my husband's boat, but it's no longer used.'

The Greek translated but Herr Becker held out his hand. '*Der Schlüssel bitte –jetzt!*' He aimed his gun at her chest.

'Please, Kyria,' the Greek wiped sweat from his forehead with his handkerchief, 'give him the key.'

Nefeli reluctantly removed the key from under the basket and told the Greek to tell Becker she would go with him. They followed her out of the taverna and along the coastline. All the time Herr Becker had his gun pointed at her. When they reached the cave, two other soldiers were already there trying to force the gate open. They moved aside as she nervously pulled the heavy chain towards her and struggled with the padlock while outwardly trying not to show the fear that churned inside her, knowing they would search every nook and cranny of the dark, damp cave.

Nefeli stood by the gate, holding her breath. The caique was still leaning against the far side of the cave where it was firmly wedged against the rocks after the watery deluge. The men turned it over, shining a flashlight over every corner checking for the smallest sign of illegal activities.

'Tell them the boat is never used,' Nefeli murmured to the Greek. 'Whatever they are looking for, they won't find it here.'

Becker scowled at her and ordered his men to search the crevices around the cave. They moved rocks and shone flashlights into the darkest of spaces and at one point were so close to where the guns and ammunition were hidden that she was sure they would be discovered. She felt her legs turning to jelly and leaned against the cave wall to steady herself. The Greek could tell she was frightened. For whatever reason, he came to her aid.

'Gentlemen, there's obviously nothing here. Let's move along the coast and see if we can find another cave.' He threw her a sympathetic look.

Becker ordered his men out, leaving Nefeli to lock up. The Greek saw her hands were trembling and helped her lock the gate.

'I've got nothing to hide,' Nefeli said, trying desperately to compose herself.

The man gave her a half-smile. 'As you say, Kyria.'

He turned and walked ahead of her, trying to catch up with the Germans. When Becker was out of sight, she called out to him.

'Who are you,' she asked, 'and why are you with these men? Are you one of those — a collaborator?'

The man swung round to face her. 'Do you think it's my choice?' he replied angrily. 'I'm from Kos. They made me help them because I speak German.'

'You seem pretty fluent to me. Where did you learn?' Nefeli was still unsure whether he was telling the truth.

'I spent several years in Germany before the war.'

He turned and hurried away but she ran after him. 'Tell me, what are they looking for?'

'Arms: there's a rumour the *andartes* have been storing stolen guns, etc., in a cave in one of the islands.'

'Where did they hear that?' Nefeli grew anxious again.

'I think someone might have talked under interrogation.'

They reached the coastal pathway and saw Herr Becker impatiently looking their way. He called out to the Greek to get a move on.

'Sorry I don't know any more.'

The Greek hurried ahead to join the Germans, leaving Nefeli behind. After a brief conversation on the beach at the same spot where Socrates used to sit mending his fishing net, they headed for a small boat which took them out to the much larger patrol boat. Nefeli was relieved to see them go. Then she noticed the Greek dropped something. She almost called out to him, but then thought better of it. She waited until they were back in the larger boat and out of sight before she went to see what it was. It was a small pocket German/Greek dictionary, and by its poor condition, had obviously been well-used. She leafed through it. On the inside cover was written in Greek, *Christos Grivas, Heidelberg, 1934.* She pocketed it and returned to the taverna to clean up the mess and pick up the spilt food off the floor. She put the book aside to look through later. It was much too precious to throw away.

Chapter 9

NEFELI LOOKED DOWN at the stranger in amazement. Every now and again, his eyes flickered open and he emitted a strange gurgling sound as though he was gasping for air. She couldn't be sure if he was in the final stages of death as she'd heard the same sounds coming from a dying man who was shot by the Germans in Chora. She and the other villagers were forced to walk past him in a single file and take note of what happened when someone defied them. The sight and the awful sound stayed with her for weeks.

'How long has he been like this?' she asked Georgia.

Georgia's voice called out from the other side of the kilim. She refused to go anywhere near him. 'Several hours. I was doing school work when I first heard him and I thought I was imagining things because it lasted barely a few seconds — and it was so soft. I was scared but peeked to take a look at him. His eyelids flickered yet he still looked the same. An hour later, he did it again. It was a horrible guttural sound and much louder. That's when I went outside and waited for you.'

Nefeli asked Georgia to get the raki from the pannier.

'He's going to live, isn't he?' Georgia said, more as a statement of fact than a question. She passed the bottle between the kilims, her head turned away to avoid looking at what lay behind them. 'I'm scared.'

Nefeli didn't reply. Georgia could hear her moving about behind the hangings and asked again. This time, Nefeli opened the kilims and tied them back to let in some light.

'Stop this at once,' she said angrily. 'I've had a terrible day and you're not making it any easier. What can he do to you?'

Georgia backed away and sat on the divan while Nefeli settled herself on the floor and attempted to pour a little raki into the man's mouth. In a matter of seconds, he gulped and spluttered and his eyes flickered open again. This time they stayed open, staring at her in a way that frightened her. It was a strange, vacant look, as if he looked beyond her to somewhere else. *Maybe he was blind.* She noticed he had beautiful eyes — the colour of the Aegean sky — blue and sparkling. She was so taken that she tipped too much raki into his mouth and he started to choke. She hastily lifted his head until he stopped. His eyes closed and he lay motionless again. Nefeli felt his pulse, as she had done frequently since she found him, and this time she was sure it was much faster.

Georgia refused to be silenced. 'He's not going to die after all, is he? What are you going to do now? I don't want to stay here alone with him. The next time you leave the house, I shall go with you.'

Nefeli covered the man with the blanket, put the raki away and joined her on the divan. 'It's still possible he may not pull through.'

Georgia knew her mother too well. 'He swallowed the raki, his heart still beats, and I think you *want* him to live.'

Nefeli fixed her eyes on Georgia, searching for something to say.

'You do, don't you?' Georgia continued, when her mother didn't reply. 'Why do you want this stranger — the enemy — to live? I am afraid the villagers will kill you if they find out.'

'The Germans were here today — at the taverna.'

'Then why didn't you tell them you'd rescued him. They would take him away and maybe...'

'Maybe what?'

'Give you a reward. Then you wouldn't have to marry again.'

Nefeli laughed. 'Oh my precious one; if only it was that simple.' The laughter faded and she became serious. 'There was a Greek with them. I think he was there under duress, but I couldn't be sure. Maybe he would tell people what we had done. Besides, the *andartes* have hidden things in caves and if they find them, we will all be in trouble. I wanted them to leave as soon as possible.'

'What have the *andartes* hidden?'

'Never you mind.'

Georgia hated it when her mother treated her like this.

'It's guns, isn't it? That's what the *andartes* have hidden.'

'Who told you that?'

'I overheard Michalis one night.'

'Please never talk like this in front of anyone.' Nefeli drew her daughter into her arms, stroking her hair. 'Promise me. We could be killed.'

'You must get rid of him, Mama.'

'I know.' Nefeli pulled German/Greek dictionary from her

pocket and showed it to her. 'Look. I found this on the beach. The Greek dropped it as they were leaving.'

'What if he realizes he lost it there and comes back for it?' Georgia said, leafing through the pages.

'That's what I was thinking.' Nefeli paused for a while deep in thought. 'It also occurred to me that if the stranger does get better, the man might be able to get him away from here without anyone knowing, and in return for us saving his life, he might use his influence and free any *andartes* in the area.'

'Do you really believe that?'

'I honestly don't know. When I saw the stranger dying in the cove, I could easily have smashed his head with a rock and dragged him to the shore to be washed back out to sea, and that would have been the end of it. No-one would have been any wiser. But my conscience wouldn't let me, and now I have to face the consequences.

*

A few days had passed since Nefeli had brought the stranger into her house and, against all odds, he was still alive. She considered this something of a miracle: maybe God meant him to live after all. Every day she had cleaned him, squeezed herbal water into his mouth in an attempt to give him nourishment, and now she set about spooning a thin, watery fish stock into his mouth too. She was doing this when Dimitri arrived to finish the roof on the outhouse. Thankfully, Georgia alerted her and the kilims were closed in time. All the same, she was careful not to invite him into the house in case the stranger made any more strange noises.

Dimitri had also brought her more fish and a few vegetables, which Nefeli was grateful for. The days were still very hot and she asked him to take a seat at the table on the terrace while she prepared them a drink and something to eat. Careful to keep the door closed, she pulled Georgia aside and told her to go to the outhouse and fetch the stranger's belongings which were hidden in a piece of cloth under a pile of rocks.

'I'll keep Dimitri occupied,' she whispered. 'He won't suspect a thing. Bring them back and hide them in there.' She pointed to the wool sack next to the loom. Georgia scowled but did as she was told.

'The Germans were here,' Nefeli said, matter-of-factly, when she and Dimitri were alone. 'They searched the cave and almost found the weapons. Did you encounter them too?'

'Yes. They came to Mikrolimano, searched around, found nothing and left.'

'Did you see the Greek who was with them?'

Dimitri wiped his mouth with the back of his hand. It never ceased to amaze Nefeli how many of the villagers had lowly table-manners. She wondered how they would fare on the larger islands or in cities like Athens and Thessaloniki.

'I've seen him before. I believe he works with the maritime authorities in Kos — something to do with the ferries. I know the Germans have taken over a nearby villa and set up a make-shift prison and interrogation centre there. From what I gather, the Germans often use him as a translator.'

'Then you know him?'

Dimitri shrugged. 'No. It's only what I heard — from other *andartes*.'

'Is he a collaborator?'

'Why do you ask?' He filled his mouth with another home-made biscuit.

Nefeli stared at the ground, afraid of giving her thoughts away to her close friend. At that moment, Georgia walked past with the man's belongings in the cloth and disappeared into the house, almost slamming the door behind her.

'Is she alright?' Dimitri asked.

'She's upset because she can't go to school. That's all. She'll get over it.' Nefeli continued the conversation. 'When they started searching the cave, I think the Greek could tell by the look on my face that I was scared. At one point, they were so close to the weapons I thought they would find them. That's when the man urged them to move on and search elsewhere.'

'The good thing is they didn't discover anything, so it's unlikely they'll look there again.' He chuckled. 'Perhaps it was your powers of persuasion that made him say that.'

Nefeli ignored the remark. 'There was a moment when we were alone and I asked him outright why he was with them. He said they used him because he spoke fluent German and he gave me the distinct feeling he was there under duress.'

'He would try and give you that idea, wouldn't he? All the Greeks working with the Germans say that.'

Dimitri thanked her for the snack, saying he'd better start work on the outhouse as he had to get back. Toula had more chores for him. While he unloaded the supplies from his mule, Nefeli returned to the house where Georgia was sitting at the table doing her homework.

Georgia indicated to the sack. 'It's safely hidden.'

Nefeli put her index finger to her mouth in a gesture which was all too clear. *This is our secret, remember.* 'Now,' she said, almost pushing Georgia out the door. 'I want you to go outside and make yourself useful to Dimitri. 'Keep an eye on him.'

Dimitri finished his work by lunchtime and left. Just as he was saying goodbye, he suddenly remembered he had to give her a message.

'Oh yes, I happened to see Kyria Eleni. She told me to tell you she has some good news for you.' He winked leaving Nefeli in no doubt as to the news.

'Please tell her I will meet her at the Blue Dolphin as arranged.'

After he left, Nefeli went back inside the house, closed the door and leaned back on it, letting out a long sigh. Georgia asked if everything was alright.

'I have a meeting with the ladies from Chora tomorrow.'

'Will I have another papa then?' She slammed her books closed and threw herself on the divan sucking on the last of Konstantinos' boiled sweets, the tears starting to roll down her cheeks.

Chapter 10

Nefeli arrived at the Blue Dolphin early enough to cook a dish of *briami* with a few of the vegetables Dimitri had given her. He'd also given her mussels which she intended to cook in a pilaf. The *briami* was almost ready when she spotted a small motor launch flying a flag with the swastika arriving in the cove. Three young men got out and strode across the beach, heading straight for the taverna. One of them had a small sack with him. Nefeli held her breath, praying there wasn't going to be a repeat of the previous visit. Fortunately, that wasn't so and, although they were armed, they had a much more pleasant attitude than the other Germans. In broken Greek, one of them asked if she could cook the fish they'd caught. She took a look in the bag. There was an assortment of delicious fresh fish including *Barbounia,* the red mullet favoured by almost every Greek when dining at a seaside taverna, and several grey mullet known as *Kefalos.* She offered to dip the red mullet in flour and fry it and the grey mullet she would stuff with herbs and lemon and cook it in the oven.

'What else is on the menu?' the men asked.

Nefeli showed them the *briami* and after a short discussion, they said they'd like to try some. Nefeli showed them the mussels too and said she was adding them to rice but that wouldn't be ready yet.

'This will be fine,' the man replied, 'and bring us a drink while we are waiting for the fish to cook.'

The men sat outside on the terrace and Nefeli served them a bottle of white wine to have with the *briami*. They appeared in good spirits, chatting away in German as if all was normal and the war was far away. For a brief moment it was. In this idyllic hideaway, with its beach taverna and perfect weather, they were making the most of it. By the time the fish was cooked and served and the third bottle of wine had been opened, the three women turned up. They eyed the Germans with contempt but Nefeli assured them it was unlikely the men would cause any trouble; they were perfect gentlemen. They took a seat at a table inside, far enough away from the Germans where they could talk in private and yet still keep an eye on them. Nefeli served the rest of the *briami*, the mussel pilaf, and a few left-over *Barbounia*.

After a while, the German who spoke Greek, came inside and offered Nefeli money for their meal. She didn't want to charge them. After all, they had brought their own fish.

'Pay whatever you like,' she said, almost apologetically. 'I'm glad you enjoyed it.'

The man looked at the three women glaring at him as if they wished him dead and smiled. 'Ladies, not all Germans are bad, you know.' He opened his wallet and placed more than enough drachmas for the meal on the table.

Nefeli's face reddened. 'That's too much, sir.'

103

'Take it.' He called to one of the other men and in German, told him to leave the rest of the fish.

Nefeli looked embarrassed. 'Sir, please…'

'We can get more.' With that he turned on his heel and the men headed for the motor launch.

Kyria Kalliope scowled. 'Do they think a smile and a sack of fish will excuse them for what they've done to us?'

Nefeli ignored her. Any fish was welcome, regardless of where it came from. She cleared the table and sat down to discuss the reason for their visit — the marriage proposal.

Kyria Angeliki took out the photos they'd brought along and one by one went through them, watching Nefeli's reaction as she handed her each picture. They had come with five proposals.

'As you can imagine,' Kyria Kalliope said, in her usual no-nonsense manner, 'with most of the young men working for Hitler in Germany, or joining the *andartes*, there aren't too many to choose from.' She sighed. 'We did our best though and can vouch for them all. They are honourable men from good families.'

Kyria Eleni and Kyria Angeliki nodded in agreement.

Nefeli looked at the first photograph, scrutinizing his face. He was much older than she had in mind, and although not too deficient in good looks, did not set her heart racing.

Kyria Kalliope sensed Nefeli's hesitation, quickly continuing the conversation with the merits of the man in question. 'He is from Kalymnos and comes from a long line of sponge divers.'

Like all the islanders, Nefeli knew of the dangers of sponge-diving. Many made several dives a day without taking breaks and hundreds died or were paralyzed due to decompression. Thousands more were permanently disabled. 'Does he still dive?' she asked.

'Not so much these days. The Germans are wary of the sponge divers. They've got it into their heads that because they can spend a longer time under water than others, they could be coerced by the *andartes* to attach mines to the ships and blow them up. He helps tend his family's goats on the mountainside instead.'

Nefeli studied the man's face. He appeared to be in his late forties with an elongated face that resembled a Byzantine icon. He had kind dark eyes 'Does he have a limp?' She was referring to the injuries caused by decompression.

The women shifted uncomfortably in their chairs.

'I believe, he does, but I've been assured it's not prominent,' Kyria Angeliki said.

'A limp is a limp,' Nefeli replied without emotion, and put the photograph to one side.

The next man was from Kos: a bar owner in his mid-fifties.

Kyria Angeliki pointed out that because he ran a bar, he agreed to allow her to keep the Blue Dolphin taverna on the condition they employed a manager to run it, which would leave her time for her 'wifely duties'. He too was cast aside.

The third was a schoolteacher from Astypalaia. He was in his mid-forties and already had six children. His photograph was placed on top of the bar owner's.

The fourth, a goatherd called Mikis from a smallholding between Chora and Mikrolimano whose family made cheese, was also cast aside. He was in his mid-fifties, had never been married, and was thought to be rather simple-minded. Nefeli let out a deep sigh and made a sharp comment saying that if that was all they could come up with, then she was not impressed. With a look of irritation that told the women they were wasting her time and theirs, she asked to see the last photograph. The women looked at each other before speaking.

'Well! Where is the photograph of the fifth man?' Nefeli asked again.

'We didn't need a photograph of this man, you already know him well,' Kyria Kalliope replied. 'It's Konstantinos Vervatis, the owner of *O Ermis* grocery store.

Nefeli's eyes widened. 'Is this some sort of joke?' she asked, tersely.

This time it was the softer-spoken Kyria Eleni who replied. 'Not at all: I happened to go to his store the same day you came to see me and he mentioned you were there buying a curtain rod. As there was no-one in the store, I told him you were thinking of taking another husband — in confidence of course.'

Nefeli felt her cheeks reddening. Kyria Eleni knew exactly what she was doing.

'He asked me to sit and have a drink with him and as I had time on my hands, I accepted. He poured us both a glass of ouzo and asked if you had any suitors. I told him there were one or two and that's when he asked me to add his name to the list. Naturally, you could have knocked me over with a feather.'

'Naturally!' Nefeli replied, with more than a hint of sarcasm.

Kyria Eleni smiled, choosing to ignore the sarcasm. 'Do you know what he told me?' Her eyes narrowed mischievously at the thought of revealing a big secret.

'I cannot possibly imagine.'

'That he had always had a soft spot for you, but your heart was only for Yianni.'

Kyria Kalliope and Kyria Angeliki joined in as if Kyria Eleni's proposal was a blessing from God Himself.

'We had cast our net far and wide, but there was our answer — right under our noses. Everyone loves Konstantinos. He is a respected man, and you cannot deny he was a good husband to his wife before her untimely death, God rest her soul,' said Kyria Angeliki. 'He and Yianni were like brothers. He respected him very much, you know.'

There were a few minutes of awkward silence and the three old women looked at one another, none of them quite knowing how to read her face. The fact that she hadn't dismissed him was a good sign.

Kyria Eleni broke the silence. 'And he loves your daughter you know — which means…' She broke off, not quite knowing what to say.

'What else did he say?' Nefeli asked. 'He might not have a wife or child of his own, but he does have a mother that he has to look after; an old battle-axe from what I gather. I don't think I could put up with her, and Georgia certainly couldn't.'

'That's true, Kyria Vervatis is a formidable woman, but she's old and doesn't have long to live. She won't be around forever: maybe a couple of years at the most. Surely that's a small price to pay for a good man — and one who is respected and quite well off. There is also another important point to consider — Konstantinos said you could keep the Blue Dolphin. He knows what it means to you because of Yianni. The two of you could run it together. The thing is though, he would like you to sell your own house and move into his house next to the shop. It's not possible for him to run the shop from your house. It's too far away. Otherwise, your life continues as it is — you will have the Blue Dolphin *and* you have security: an agreeable outcome.'

Nefeli mulled Konstantinos' proposal over in her mind. Now it all began to make sense: the sweets he gave to Georgia, the occasional extras he'd put in a bag for her which she'd never asked for, the times she'd bought something and paid him back later because money had been tight. Now she understood it wasn't just because he was a friend. Any other man would have made his intentions known long before now, but Konstantinos was not that kind of man. He was, as the three women pointed out, a good man, and Yianni had liked him too, which was something in his favour. The three women could sense Nefeli was warming to the idea.

'I must discuss it with Georgia,' Nefeli said. 'I promised her I wouldn't take another man that she didn't approve of.'

Kyria Kalliope threw her hands in the air. '*Aman*! She's still a child. You must decide what is best for her.'

Nefeli got up to clear the table. 'Thank you, ladies. I will let you know my answer tomorrow. Now, if you don't mind, I have work to do. I want to salt the rest of this fish before it goes off.'

'What do we tell Konstantinos?' Kyria Eleni said. 'He will surely be looking out for us when we return.'

'Tell him, he will have my answer soon.'

Chapter 11

THE STRANGER HAD been quiet all day. No strange gurgling sounds. No gasps of breath. Nothing: just a deathly silence and Nefeli was even more convinced he would die at any moment. No-one could last that long in such a state and without nourishment. She finally had to admit that they'd have to bury him and began to think of somewhere he could be laid to rest without being disturbed, somewhere the villagers would not take revenge and desecrate his final resting place.

After preparing left-over fish and rice for Georgia's supper, Nefeli suggested they eat it on the terrace. She had something important she wanted to discuss with her. The intense heat of the day was replaced with a cool sea-breeze that gently rolled inland, bringing a taste of the Aegean with it. After they'd finished the meal, they sat for a while watching the sun go down and Nefeli told her about Konstantinos' proposal. She omitted to tell her about the other four men she'd quickly dismissed without a second thought, or that Konstantinos wanted them to move to Chora.

Georgia listened but as much as she tried, she was too young to grasp the enormity of the situation.

'What do you think, *agapi mou*?' Nefeli asked, watching her daughter as she picked up the cat that had been purring at her feet and started stroking it. 'You like him, don't you?' Without waiting for an answer, she continued, trying hard to soften the bad news. 'And your father liked him too. They were good friends, you know.'

Georgia thought about the times Konstantinos had called her over to his shop after school and given her a few sweets. Had he been kind just because he liked her mother? Whatever his reason, she thought him a nice man.

'Will you love him, Mama? Like you did Papa?'

'If he is good to us, then I will grow to love him.'

Nefeli knew in her heart it would be a different kind of love: one born out of respect which the Greeks considered more enduring. When she thought about it, she and Yianni were the exception to the rule. They were madly in love from the start. For a while, they sat in silence, both lost in their own thoughts. There was little more to be said. The announcement of Konstantinos as the new husband and father in their lives was accepted with little emotion. This was their fate and they would get on with it.

Nefeli got up to clear the plates and went back inside. The announcement had taken Georgia by surprise and she sat outside until the sun slipped over the horizon before returning to the house.

'If that's what you want, Mama, then I am happy too.' She undressed and got into bed, but Nefeli couldn't fail to notice the tears that glistened in her daughter's sad eyes.

She waited until she was fast asleep before warming up the fish broth to drip feed the stranger as she had become accustomed to every morning and evening. She placed a candle on the floor behind the kilims and sat beside him as she always did, gently lifting his head and tilting it to one side to spoon a little broth into his mouth. It would probably be the last time she would do this. A part of her was relieved, as hiding him was a huge burden, yet at the same time, she would miss him. That mixture of emotions confused her. She stroked his face and ran her fingers through his hair in between slipping the broth between his lips. With every spoonful, a little dribbled and she wiped it tenderly with a hand-towel.

Poor soul; you have a family somewhere. They will never know what happened to you. I will light a candle and pray for you — and for them too. This cruel war destroys us all.

What came over her next took her by complete surprise. She felt a sudden urge to kiss him and leaned forward and kissed his forehead. He was warm and smelt good, partly because of her wiping his brow daily with fragrant water, and partly because he was a man. His smell reminded her of Yianni. Instead of pulling back, her eyes fell on his mouth, beautifully shaped and full of passion. She imagined them moving when he spoke. Had he spoken words of love? Without thinking, she pressed her lips on them. In that moment, a strange, sweet feeling of compassion and sensuality took hold of her; a thousand thoughts condensed into that one kiss. The feel of her lips against his felt so good. She closed her eyes and for a brief moment, experienced an emotion that not even the greatest of poets could describe. Yianni used to tell her that lovers were like flames that ignited the universe, showering the world with a myriad of bright stars. Whatever it was, it aroused a passion she'd kept locked away for too long. Memories of him flooded her mind and she found herself weeping. It was as if her very soul had stopped feeling since his death, and now she'd awoken as if from a long sleep.

A tear fell on his lips, as salty as the fish broth she had been trying to give him. It was all so silly, so unreal — and so very painful. She pulled back, stunned at her actions and immediately crossed herself, asking the Virgin to forgive her for committing such a terrible sin. Her head was spinning and she was exhausted. Rather than get up and sleep in the main room, she simply pulled a pillow from the marital bed, covered herself with a light coverlet and fell asleep on the floor next to the stranger.

In the middle of the night, she woke with a start. She felt a fleeting sensation of something brushing against her hand. At first, she thought it was Georgia, but the kilims were still closed and she was asleep. The room was in darkness. She'd been so tired, she'd fallen asleep with the candle burning and it had burnt itself out, leaving behind a pool of sweet-smelling beeswax in a saucer. The moon was on the wane, a silver sliver in the night sky giving barely any light at all and forcing her to grope around in the darkness for a small box in which she kept more candles. There was one left, partly used with only a few centimetres left. She lit it, praying the flame would last. As it spluttered into life, she felt it again. It was barely perceptible, yet she was sure something touched her. *Surely it couldn't be a rat? That's why they had the cat and he was a good hunter.* After attaching the candle onto the melted beeswax in the saucer, she moved to stand up, embarrassed that she'd fallen asleep on the floor. *What if Georgia had found her like that? The poor child would have got the fright of her life.*

The candle cast a warm, hallowed glow on the whitewashed walls, highlighting the Virgin's face near the marital bed. Cautiously, she turned and held it closer to the stranger's face and immediately pulled back in horror, clutching the edge of the dowry chest and almost dropping the candle. His eyes were open and he was staring at her! She scuttled in terror as far away from him as the small room would allow, but something jerked her back. She'd caught her skirt on something. She tugged hard and when she lowered the candle to see what it was, saw the man's hand and realized he was grasping it. Shaking in terror, she quickly put down the candle and tried to prize open his hand. By now, his eyes were closed again but his fingers were locked in such a tight grasp, she had to forcibly wrench each finger away until she was free. She picked up the spluttering candle and, almost tripping over him, burst through the kilims into the main room and grabbed a knife.

Throughout all this, Georgia slept soundly, but for Nefeli, a good night's sleep was now impossible. She sat at the table, shaking like a leaf and holding the knife as tightly as the stranger had held her skirt. After a while, when she was sure there was no movement from the marital chamber, she laid her head on her hands, drifting in and out of a light sleep filled with nightmares of being interrogated and ending up before a firing squad.

In the morning she felt something tugging at her arm and woke with a scream, brandishing the knife in front of her. When she realised it was only Georgia, who stepped back quickly when saw her mother pointing the knife at her, she dropped it on the table and clasped her hands to her face, stifling a cry of distress.

'Mama! What's happened? You're frightening me.'

Nefeli jumped up and peeked behind the kilims. The stranger was still lying there in the same position with his eyes closed. She pulled her daughter into her arms, holding her so tightly that Georgia struggled to free herself crying out loudly. 'You're hurting me!'

'I was so tired that I must have had a bad dream. I thought he was attacking me.'

The combination of lack of sleep and worry about their future was beginning to take its toll and she told Georgia to get ready; they were going to Chora to meet with Kyria Eleni.

Chapter 12

NEFELI LEFT GEORGIA with a friend while she went to see Kyria Eleni. The old woman had been expecting her and had prepared a platter of dried fruits and freshly baked biscuits to celebrate the upcoming marriage which she had no doubt, would be announced to everyone before sundown that day.

'What did the girl say?' Kyria Eleni asked, as she poured the coffee into the small porcelain cups.

'She approves,' Nefeli replied. She wasn't sure if Georgia really did approve but there was no point discussing that now. They had started the ball rolling and there was no going back.

'She's a good girl and he will take care of her.' Kyria Eleni slid the coffee towards her and glanced at the clock. 'They should be here any minute now.'

'They?'

'I invited Konstantinos, and Kyria Vervatis asked to come along too.' There was a knock on the door. 'Ah, that must be them now.' She got up to greet them.

'Come in, come in.' Kyria Eleni's face beamed as if she were about to give her own daughter away.

Kyria Vervatis, a small, thin woman dressed from head to toe in black, shuffled forward, followed by her only son, resplendent in his best suit and tie regardless of the fact that the sun was beating down. Nefeli stood up and planted a kiss on his mother's cheek. The old woman had the wizened features of an old crone and her eyes were dull and lifeless, which Nefeli surmised was probably due to many years of unhappiness. She acknowledged Nefeli with a nod and sat down on a chair with a soft cushion which Kyria Eleni plumped up vigorously, more as a gesture of trying to win her over than genuine concern for her frail body.

Konstantinos presented Nefeli with a bunch of wildflowers wrapped in newspaper and a box of Turkish Delight to share with Georgia.

'*Kalimera*, Nefeli.'

Nefeli felt her cheeks redden. '*Kalimera*,' she replied, barely able to look at him.

She could see he was just as embarrassed as she was and after an uncomfortable silence, Kyria Eleni stated the obvious — the reason they were gathered together. Konstantinos spoke next, directing his words to Nefeli.

'When I heard you were thinking of taking another husband, I confess, my heart soared and I was more than happy to add my name to your list of suitors. As you know, I loved my wife dearly — and of course, Yianni — but I have always had feelings for you, feelings I might add, that have sometimes been hard to control.'

Kyria Eleni studied Nefeli's reaction. The women had been right when they said she turned men's head with her beauty and they had done well to bring the situation to a head.

Konstantinos continued, oblivious to Kyria Eleni's thoughts. 'When Kyria Eleni told me you had considered me favourably as a suitor, I was elated.' Nefeli blushed. Their conversations had always been brusque –almost business-like, and now here he was, speaking the language of poets. 'I know you have a child and I will be a good father to her. She is a sweet girl. Perhaps God will see fit to bless us with more children and she will have brothers and sisters. It's not good for a child to be alone.'

Kyria Eleni nodded in agreement. Nefeli, on the other hand, did not consider Georgia to be *alone* as he put it. Neither did she want more children. At that point, Kyria Eleni and Kyria Vervatis took over. They wanted the finer points of the marriage settlement sorted out before they went any further. Nefeli cringed at the way the meeting took on a business-like tone. Kyria Vervatis said she'd already seen her dowry possessions: the embroideries, carpets, jewellery and trinkets, etc., when she married Yianni. All the women on the island had come to pay their respects and look over the bride's dowry. Now she was interested in the accumulated wealth since his death. In other words, what else of monetary significance would she bring to the marriage? After all, as she pointed out, her son was still a desirable match and finding another wife with good prospects would not be hard, especially with half the male population killed or missing due to the war.

It was established that the Blue Dolphin taverna was worth quite a lot of money, but with a war on, it might be better closing it down so that Nefeli could help Konstantinos in the store. They could always sell the taverna when times improved. She also suggested she could utilize her business expertise to extend *O*

117

Ermis into a *kafeneio* as it occupied an excellent position in the square.

Then there was the house which Nefeli was reluctant to part with. It was impossible for them to travel backwards and forwards to Chora every day so she would have to vacate it. Like the taverna, selling it seemed a near impossibility at the moment but Nefeli stressed she did not want to sell it. After a heated discussion, Konstantinos came to Nefeli's defence and pacified his mother by saying they might use it every now and again as a second home and more importantly, it could be used for Georgia's dowry.'

'Is there anything else?' Kyria Vervatis asked, casting her eyes over the list Kyria Eleni had written down. 'Didn't you have a boat? What happened to it?'

The boat was something Nefeli never spoke about except with members of the *andartes*. 'It hasn't been used since Yianni went away and I'm not even sure it's seaworthy any longer,' she replied. 'If it was, I would go out and catch fish myself.'

Nefeli knew this to be a lie. Michalis had told her that because it was kept out of water and safe from the elements, it was still usable. Even so, she didn't want anyone going anywhere near the cave while weapons were stored there. It reminded her that she must get Dimitri to move them somewhere else now that their friends were no longer around.

There were a few other minor issues to discuss and after two long hours, the meeting drew to a close. The wedding was to take place at the church in Chora in three weeks' time. It was also agreed that the two would not meet again until the wedding; the villagers were apt to gossip and make trouble and no-one wanted that. Nefeli must be beyond reproach. The four celebrated with a glass of Kyria Eleni's pomegranate liqueur which she kept for special occasions. After all, this was certainly something worth celebrating, not merely because of the impending marriage, but because Kyria Eleni and her two friends' status in the community as excellent marriage-brokers would be firmly established. Work like this brought gifts — usually a considerable amount of money, fine embroideries, or jewellery, depending on what the family could provide. Against all odds, their persistence had finally paid off. With the beautiful Nefeli firmly under her new husband's care, the lustful eyes of every other man on the island would stop wandering. Yes, this was definitely worth celebrating. Kyria Eleni refilled their glass and they drank to the happy union.

Konstantinos' face shone with happiness. 'Thank you,' he whispered to Nefeli, his voice filled with emotion. 'You have made me a happy man. I only hope you feel the same way.'

Nefeli assured him she did, but the ever-vigilant eyes of his mother noticed she looked at the ground when she answered.

Holding her bunch of flowers, Nefeli walked away to collect Georgia. Her eyes were so full of tears she could barely see. This should have been a happy occasion but throughout the journey back home, neither Nefeli nor Georgia uttered a word. Nefeli was so tired she could barely think. *Had she done the right thing by agreeing to marry Konstantinos? She didn't even love him!* When she looked into his eyes, she felt nothing.

The closer they neared the house, the more thoughts of what took place the night before began to plague her. The stranger must be dead by now, she told herself, and they would have to bury him during the night. In this heat a body deteriorated fast. She'd experienced it far too often in the past and it was a distressing sight. The smell was worse than rotting fish and she didn't want Georgia to experience that on top of everything else.

Before long, the path meandered through the olive grove, giving them a full view of the house. Nefeli had been careful to bolt the shutters and lock the door. When the terrace came into view, something caught her eye. She stopped and jerked her hand out, cautioning Georgia not to move. Her heart pounding, she saw that the shutters were still closed, but the door leading to the terrace was wide open. Something was dreadfully wrong.

Chapter 13

Nefeli told Georgia to stay where she was while she went to investigate.

'Stay behind this tree in the shadow and don't move until I call you.'

Trembling like a leaf, Georgia crouched down on the earth begging her mother to take care but Nefeli was already out of earshot. The open door had shocked her out of her lethargy and finding a renewed energy she picked up a rock and a large stick to defend herself and ran towards the house. Reaching the terrace, she approached the open door with caution and checked the area before entering. There was no-one in sight. From where she stood, she had a clear view of the two kilims. They were still closed, just as she had left them. Inching her way inside, she exchanged the rock for the knife she'd used the night before and quietly moved aside one of the curtains. The stranger had vanished.

She fell back against the wall, letting out a loud gasp. '*Theé mou!*'

But God wasn't going to help her. In a panic, she ran to the door, scanning the landscape once more but he was nowhere in sight. She called out to Georgia to come quickly.

'He's gone!' Nefeli said. 'How can a man who was at death's door suddenly get up and disappear?'

She thought of the many miracles the islanders had talked about: people returning from the dead, illnesses that were cured overnight. There were so many. Her eyes fell on a piece of paper torn out of a notebook that lay near the German/Greek dictionary on the table.

'What's this? It wasn't here before.' On it was written in Greek, *s'efcharistó*.

She stared at it in disbelief and showed it to Georgia. The stranger had written *thank you*. 'He can't have gone very far. I have to find him before the villagers spot him first. God only knows what will happen if they do.'

She stuffed the note in her pocket and ran outside with Georgia tugging at her skirt. 'Mama: no! Please don't go. It's dangerous.'

'Do you really think a man who leaves a thank-you note will do us harm? Besides, he's still injured so he can't be too far away — and he hasn't any shoes. Stay here and lock yourself in the house.'

Nefeli jerked her skirt free and ran from the house towards the sea thinking that was the most likely place he would go to catch the attention of one of the many German patrol boats that passed by on a regular basis. Within a matter of minutes, she reached the rocks leading to Aphrodite's Cove where she'd first discovered him and stood at a point which gave her a good view of the cove, but there was still no sign of him. She made a quick decision to head left in the direction of the taverna, perhaps because the path was more well-trodden making it easier to walk along for someone without shoes. At a certain point where the waves washed rhythmically over a series of rocks jutting out into the sea, she caught a glimpse of something white against one of the rocks below. Rather than follow the winding path, she jumped from one rock to another like an agile mountain goat. Seconds later she saw him, sprawled out on the sand below with his back cushioned against rock and a thick tussock of sea grass. She stood for a few moments watching him, the knife clenched tightly in her hand. He, on the other hand, edged himself into a sitting position and smiled at her. It was a tired smile, tinged with pain, but a smile nevertheless. Nefeli's heart was beating fast. Her mind was telling her she should plunge the knife into him before he had time to think — but no — she didn't wish him dead at all. In fact, she was happy he was alive.

Steadying himself with one arm, he raised his other towards her in a gesture of submission. Nefeli walked slowly toward him and stood near his feet looking down at him, the knife in readiness to defend herself. All the time their eyes focused on each other, neither knowing what the other would do.

'S'efcharistó,' he said with a half-smile.

Nefeli did not reciprocate the smile and her reply was brusque. 'You speak Greek?'

'I studied it at university.' He moved his position, trying to get more comfortable. 'The rest I picked up while being stationed here,' he added. His face contorted in pain.

She pulled the crumpled note out of her pocket. 'You write Greek too?'

He shook his head. 'Not really. I saw the dictionary and copied the words.'

Nefeli was still shaking, but now it was more in anger. 'What a gentleman,' she said, angrily. 'My daughter and I risk our lives to save you and all you can do is write a note and leave. I ought to kill you.' She moved forward, ready to stab him.

The man put his hand up to stop her. 'You have a daughter?' He looked surprised.

'Yes,' Nefeli replied, 'and I put her at risk — for you — a German — the enemy.'

'I... I'm sorry.'

At that moment, he grimaced and slumped over. Nefeli wasn't sure if he was trying to fool her and kicked one of his feet. He didn't move. She slipped the knife into her belt and crouched down beside him, slapping his face several times. She wanted to throw water on his face to revive him, but that was impossible: she had no container and she'd never be able to drag him near the water. She slapped him again. This time it was so hard, his body jerked into a spasm and his eyes opened. She pulled back but he was too quick for her and grabbed her wrist.

'Help me!' His body was shaking and he was sweating profusely. He pointed to his chest and twisted his hand, making a snapping sound and she realised he was telling her his ribs were broken.

Rather than leave him as he was, Nefeli struggled to get him back into a sitting position. His head fell onto her shoulder and his eyes flickered. He reached for her hand and held it tight.

'Help me,' he uttered again, this time in a barely audible voice.

In the next moment she found herself cradling him, looking

down at his golden blonde hair, wet with sweat. She let go of his hand and stroked his forehead. 'You will die if you stay here,' she said in a whisper. 'You're not strong enough to go on. Do you understand?'

Nefeli was not sure if he really understood what she was saying and pointed out to sea. 'Over there is Kos. You want to go to Kos? Is that it?'

He nodded weakly.

'Not now. In a few days — when you are well.'

She knelt in front of him, cupping his face with both hands. His eyes were so blue, so clear, and so beautiful. Her eyes fell on his mouth again, just as they had over the past few days and nights. This time it was different; they had life in them. He was the enemy, but in that moment she saw in his face, the same beauty she had seen earlier. Now she felt something else — empathy. She recalled what the German had said to her at the taverna when he gave her the fish. *Not all Germans are bad, you know.*

Slowly she brought her lips closer to his and kissed them — the same tender kiss she'd given him when he was unconscious. It momentarily revived him and this time they looked into each other's eyes. She was playing a dangerous game, yet at the same time a thrill of the unknown sent tingles down her spine. The kiss seemed to linger forever until he drew back, wiped his brow in pain and starting mumbling in German. She realised he was slipping into unconsciousness again and helped lay him down on the sand.

'It's okay. You'll be fine.'

She kicked off her shoes, ran to the shore, and waded into the water. Moments later she was back by his side, ringing the seawater from her skirt over his face, careful this time that he didn't swallow any. It revived him for a while.

He struggled in vain to keep his eyes open. She sat by his side watching over him until the sun slipped over the horizon and darkness fell. When she shook him he didn't stir. In the end she stood up and kicked his foot again. It was so hard, he jolted his head back. In that split second, the anguish on his face told Nefeli he'd momentarily forgotten where he was.

'Listen to me,' she said sternly. 'It's not possible for you to stay here. You are too ill. I am taking you back to my house. If I leave you here, you will die.'

It was a struggle, but she eventually got him to his feet and slowly he took a few steps without falling down. After a few more steps, the circulation in his body improved and, with Nefeli's help and constant words of encouragement, he was able to make his way back to the house. Georgia saw her mother through the window returning with the stranger and was so frightened she refused to open the door. It took a few minutes before her mother could coax her to open it again. When she did, she backed herself against the farthest side of the room watching in disbelief as her mother led him to the divan.

'For the moment you will sleep here,' Nefeli told him, helping him get comfortable.

He thanked her, this time in German, and closed his eyes.

'Where did you find him?' Georgia asked.

'He was near Aphrodite's Cove. God knows how he had the strength to make it. He must have been very fit before the accident to have survived this. He seems to think some of his ribs are broken, but at least we know he will live now.'

Georgia noticed her mother's skirt was wet and asked what happened but Nefeli didn't reply. She knew the idea that she'd purposely tried to save him wouldn't sit well with her.

'Does he speak Greek?' Georgia asked.

'He said he studied it at university before the war.' She frowned. 'He was in too much pain to communicate clearly, but it was enough for me to understand that he'd intended to attract the attention of a patrol boat and get to Kos. Unfortunately, he collapsed and slipped between the rocks before he could make it to the shore.'

'You should have left him there.'

'Maybe, but what if the islanders had spotted him first?'

There was a pause while the pair sat at the table watching him and wondering what to do next.

'We must help him,' Nefeli said. 'Let's give him a few days to get stronger and then he can go. Maybe those kind Germans will return and I can let them know he's here. They will look favourably on us.'

Georgia frowned. 'What about the villagers? They won't.'

'The villagers don't come here. No-one comes here.'

'Dimitri and Toula do.'

'Dimitri has done all he can fixing things up after the storm. If anyone wants me, they will go to the Blue Dolphin.' Nefeli went into the marital chamber to get a fresh sheet to cover the stranger and asked Georgia to take the kilim and sheet he had been using outside to air on the terrace.

That night, Nefeli and Georgia slept together in the marital bed, just as they had done since Yianni left. Secure by her mother's side, Georgia slept better than she had in a while.

Chapter 14

THE STRANGER AND Georgia were still asleep when Nefeli got up to feed the animals and wash a few clothes outside. Already the sun's rays were casting a warm, golden glow over the island and the clothes would dry in no time. Rather than discard the precious water, she threw it over the kilim and began to wash it with a brush and olive oil soap, refilled the pan with more water to rinse the suds away, and laid it over the rocks to dry. When she turned to go back inside, the stranger was standing in the doorway watching her.

'*Theé mou*,' Nefeli said, taking a step back. 'You gave me a fright.'

'*Guten Morgen.*'

'*Kalimera.*'

She quickly ushered him inside, closed the door and shook her finger at him. 'Please don't go outside.' Then she made a gesture of slitting her throat. 'The islanders — they will kill you!'

She pointed to the table indicating for him to take a seat while she prepared a simple breakfast of dried rusks, cheese and honey. She noticed that he still limped, although she'd already ascertained his leg wasn't broken.

She placed the food on the table and sat down across from him. 'Eat,' she said, 'to get stronger.'

Nefeli was about to drizzle honey on the cheese when the man extended his hand. 'Martin,' he said, waiting for her to shake his hand. 'Martin Tristan Werner Heindorf.'

Nefeli blushed. They had kissed without even exchanging names. It was unthinkable.

'Nefeli,' she replied, shaking his hand. 'Nefeli Stellakis.' At that moment, Georgia peered between the kilims. 'Come here, *agape mou.* It's alright.'

Georgia entered the room cautiously, barely able to look the stranger in the eyes. Nefeli clasped her in her arms assuring her that she was safe. The man extended his hand to her but Georgia turned away.

'His name is Martin, my darling. Tell him your name.' Georgia refused to speak so Nefeli spoke for her.

'Georgia — a pretty name for a pretty girl,' Heindorf said in German.

Nefeli and Georgia had no idea what he'd just said, but Nefeli could tell by the way he said it, that it was probably something charming. Georgia, on the other hand, was fearful and buried her face in her mother's shoulder. The only words of German they knew were *schnell* and *raus*– words they wanted to forget because they were often accompanied by gunshots or women shrieking while their menfolk were being transported away in trucks to God knows where.

'Please don't speak in German,' Nefeli said sternly, 'especially in front of her.'

Heindorf apologised.

After they'd eaten, Nefeli went outside with Georgia while Heindorf lay down on the divan again. They needed to discuss their next move.

'We must carry on as normal — as if he wasn't here,' Nefeli said, jerking her head in the direction of the house, 'so I want you to go back to school. They've found a replacement teacher and from what I hear, she's not very good, but the point is, it's important that you go to Chora as often as possible. I want you to keep your ears open in case you hear anything — you know — about whether anyone suspects his presence.'

'What will you do, Mama?'

'I'll go to the taverna as I usually do.'

They also discussed their new sleeping arrangements. 'Until he is ready to leave, which won't be long now, he can sleep in the marital bed. That way, if anyone calls, he will be hidden. I don't want him on the floor any longer: he has to have proper sleep to get well. You and I will continue to share the divan. I know it's cramped but we'll manage.'

'What will we do about... him? He might disappear again.'

'Don't worry. I will tell him he must stay inside. I've already made it clear he could be killed.'

'Did he understand you and does he believe you? '

'I think so. His Greek seems quite good to me. It was probably a natural reaction for him to try and escape yesterday as he had no idea where he was, but I believe he now knows we've risked our necks to save him. In return for that, I don't believe he will consciously put us at risk.' She paused. 'Despite being a German, he seems a decent man and I think he will do what I ask.'

'I hope you're right.'

'Give me a kiss, sweet one — and go and get ready for school. We must make every day look like a normal day.'

After Georgia left, Nefeli prepared to leave herself. Heindorf was asleep again. She put fresh sheets on the marital bed and woke him up.

'Here,' she said, referring to the divan, 'is not good. Somebody could see you.' She showed him the marital bed and told him he could sleep there.

She also told him she was going out — to the taverna — and except for relieving himself in the hole that passed for a toilet a few metres from the house, he must stay inside. She grabbed the dictionary and choosing a few words, told him he could go out for a walk at night when it was dark. Heindorf understood everything she was saying and reminded her again that he'd studied Greek at university.

'Don't worry. I will take care,' he said.

'Good.' Nefeli replied. 'Good man.' She counted on her fingers. 'In one or two days, I will help you get to Kos.'

When she was convinced he understood the precarious position they were in, she laid out another change of clothes on the divan for him and brought inside a bucket filled with soapy water, indicating he should wash himself. After showing him where the food was kept, saying he could eat whatever he wanted, she grabbed her shawl and left, leaving the door unlocked this time.

Chapter 15

Martin Tristan Werner Heindorf was 30 years old and married with a young daughter when he joined the Luftwaffe in 1937. A promising pilot, he moved to the newly formed German 10th Air Corps, otherwise known as X *Fliegerkorps*, on 3 September 1939, based at Blankenese under the command of Generalleutnant Hans Ferdinand Geisler. Heindorf's family were from Lübeck and the fact that the Corps was stationed near Hamburg, suited him well as it was not far away from his home town. In early 1941, he was transferred to Sicily to support the build-up of the Afrika Korps in Libya. After many successful operations in the Mediterranean, he eventually found himself stationed in Greece. The Corps was crucial in securing air superiority and German victory against the Allies during the 1943 Dodecanese Campaign, and afterwards, was put under the commanding general of the German Luftwaffe in Greece in March 1944.

Sitting on the window seat looking outside beyond the rocks to a sliver of blue sea on the horizon, he thought about how much had taken place over the past few months. All that fighting against the Allies, but in the end they had won. The Dodecanese Islands were now firmly in German hands after the Italian surrender. He realised how terrified Nefeli and her daughter would have been, knowing the bombing that was taking place on the nearby islands, not to mention the dogfights they would have seen.

He moved to a more comfortable position. The excruciating stabbing pains in his chest still persisted and his hip throbbed after he slipped on the rocks. He had no idea how long he'd been here on this island. He wasn't even sure what it was called or how big it was. All he could remember was that he had been on the patrol boat following a larger boat which was blown up, presumably by the *andartes*. They were on their way to Leros where he was to pick up his airplane which was undergoing maintenance when their searchlights spotted a small boat fleeing the area and they pursued it. Whoever was on that boat stood no chance against the bigger German guns, and it sank within minutes. Then the storm hit. Martin Heindorf was used to bad weather as X *Fliegerkorps* was designed specifically for coastal operations, but this storm was different. He wasn't particularly superstitious or religious, yet in that moment he found himself praying hard. The patrol boat started to sink and two lifeboats were lowered. It all happened so fast, he couldn't even recall who was with him. The last thing he remembered was a huge tidal wave lifting the lifeboat up towards the heavens followed by an almighty crash. After that everything went blank.

Alone in the house, the silence interrupted by the occasional bird call and the sound of cicadas, he thought about the woman — Nefeli. She didn't tell him how long he'd been in her house or where she'd found him, but it was evident there wasn't a man in the house. He wouldn't have survived if there had been. He remembered waking from what seemed like a long, deep sleep and finding himself lying on the floor wearing another man's clothes. *What happened to his own clothes?* In that strange twilight state between consciousness and unconsciousness, he was aware of someone lying next to him. His hand reached out and touched something soft — her skirt. He knew it was a woman when she lit the candle. She looked frightened and he longed to say it was alright — that he wouldn't hurt her — but try as he might, the words would not come and he slipped back into the void.

The next day he woke up again but the pain was so intense he drifted in and out of consciousness for a while. At some point during the day, he managed to drag himself up off the floor and moved aside one of the heavy carpets dividing the two rooms to get a clearer view of his surroundings: a village house like none he'd ever been in before. He called out, but there was no answer. From the window he had a clear view of the rocky, windswept landscape that seemed incapable of supporting anyone except for a few goats. The house stood alone with no other building in sight. If he was going to escape, he had to do it straight away before the occupants came back. He stumbled to the door and found it locked. The pain was so severe, he almost fainted again. He grabbed hold of the chair by the table and sat down to take a few deep breaths. It was then that he saw the German/Greek dictionary on the table. As a student, his Greek had been quite good, and since being stationed in Greece he'd picked it up again quite quickly, but he couldn't write it. He flicked through the pages until he found the words he was looking for and, seeing a notebook nearby, ripped out a page and wrote the words *Thank you*. Then he picked the lock and headed in the direction of the water.

Racked with pain, he'd almost made it to the rocks when he was overcome by nausea. His head was spinning and he felt himself sliding into unconsciousness. With nothing to hold on to, he passed out, slipping down the rocks onto the sand below. Sometime later he was confronted by a woman standing in front of him and holding a knife. He stared at her in disbelief. Such a beautiful creature — and yet she looked as if she was about to plunge the knife into his heart.

Except for his wife, Emmy, and a childhood sweetheart, Martin Heindorf had not known other women, at least not physically, but he was good at reading faces and gestures. The woman was tough, there was little doubt about that, yet at the same time, he sensed vulnerability in her; she didn't want to kill him — she wanted to help him. He saw it in her eyes, dark and almond shaped, framed with long dark lashes and perfectly arched eyebrows. At the same time, he saw a fierce pride. He couldn't take his eyes off her. He was drowning in those eyes and he didn't care.

He was in no position to fight and if he was honest, he didn't even want to. He remembered her coming closer to him, her honeyed skin glistening with perspiration. The closer she got, the more her scent overpowered him. It was the scent of a woman in the prime of her life, a full-blooded woman who was not ashamed of her body. When she leaned over to help him, the swell of her bosom drew closer to his face — intoxicating, radiating a sexuality he'd never experienced before. When she smiled, he knew then that he'd fallen under her spell — Nefeli with the beautiful dark eyes. His senses numbed, not only from the pain, but from years of war, he felt as if his soul had come alive again. What happened next was a blur. All he recalled was that he passed out again and when she woke him up it was dark. She knew he wanted to escape but told him it was impossible. He was in no state to argue and she helped him back to her house.

Now he was alone again in this strange house. He had no idea where Nefeli had gone. She mentioned something about a taverna, but where was it? He noted that she'd sent her daughter to school, but where was that too? There wasn't another building in sight. It crossed his mind that they might alert the other islanders, but he quickly dismissed this. If she was going to do that, she'd have done it before now. He got up and attempted to walk up and down the room for a while in an effort to get stronger. After ten minutes he opened a large tin filled with dry rusks, took one out and smothered it in a soft white cheese. He was ravenous, a sign that he was on the way back to recovery. His eyes scanned the room. It was a simple and humble dwelling, spotlessly clean and tidy. A great deal of thought had been put into the design and decoration. His eyes fell on the wall paintings with the seascape and dolphins. They were naïve and stylistic but beautifully painted. Nothing here resembled his villa back in Lübeck, with its many rooms filled with family portraits in oil and fine furniture. That was a world away.

The loom in the corner of the house and the sacks of wool nearby intrigued him. He'd seen looms like this in Crete and watched the women deftly weave fine patterns on them, commenting on their beauty. He'd even thought of getting something to send home to Emmy but at this stage in the war, doubted it would ever get there. He helped himself to another rusk before exploring the house some more. Nefeli had told him he must sleep in her bed. It didn't take much for him to see it was the marital bed. It was tucked under an arched ceiling and one side butted up against the wall which had a small window looking out onto what appeared to be an olive and fruit orchard. There as a niche in the wall which held a candle, and a small silver icon and photograph had been placed over the bed. He studied the man in the photograph and presumed he was her husband. Where was he? There were no photographs of her daughter, Georgia, a shy child who seemed extremely close to her mother. He hadn't seen his own daughter, Hannelore, in almost four years and it made him realise how much he missed her. She would be nine soon and he would miss another birthday.

His face still ached and he examined it in a mirror on the wall. He looked terrible, bruised and with a beard that must have been at least a week old. He walked about some more until faintness forced him to lie down again. In a day or two, he would be gone, hopefully back to Kos where he could recuperate in the German hospital there, and all this would have been a dream.

Chapter 16

ALL DAY, NEFELI kept an eye out for the Germans who had called by before. She decided that if she saw the same kind man who'd left the fish, she would tell him one of their own was safe and arrange for them to pick him up in Aphrodite's Cove. She still couldn't decide whether the Greek was a collaborator though. Throughout the day she had several customers, the first being a group of old men from Chora who decided they wanted a change of scenery. They drank several glasses of ouzo and stayed for a couple of hours playing *tavli*. There was also a boat filled with sponge divers from Kalymnos who were doing the rounds selling their sponges. As she served them baked vegetables and fried fish from the fish Dimitri had given her, she listened to their conversations. It wasn't good news. Since the Italians had gone, the Germans had cracked down on the remaining Jews living in the Dodecanese Islands, and they were casting their nets far and wide. Prior to this, the Italians had not been so harsh with the Jews but rumours had circulated for a while about Greek Jews fleeing east to escape the deportations to places few Greeks had heard of until now, places like Auschwitz-Birkenau and Bergen-Belsen. She recalled Michalis and the others had taken part in escape operations, but they never told her who they helped or where they went to.

When the customers had gone, Nefeli sat on the terrace sorting through the rice and dried pulses that were scattered on the floor during the earlier German raid, waiting for Georgia to return from school. All the time her eyes scanned the water for a German patrol boat, but none came. She put the tray of food aside, took off her sandals and went for a walk along the beach, sitting for a while at the spot where Socrates used to keep his boat. How she missed him, a wise old soul with so many stories to tell. The sun was beating down and the sand was hot. The clear blue water looked inviting and she longed to take a dip to cool off. She was about to do just that when she heard Georgia call from the terrace.

'How was it?' Nefeli asked while making her a drink of freshly squeezed lemon juice. 'How was the new teacher?'

'She's kind and I like her. She gave us some Greek language and history exercises and sat at her desk reading the newspaper until we'd finished. At the end of the lesson, she called each of us up and asked us to tell her about ourselves.'

Nefeli was concerned. 'Why would she do that? What did she want to know?'

'Where we lived, how many brothers and sisters we had, what our fathers did; things like that.'

The first thing that came into Nefeli's mind was that she was a spy — a collaborator sent by the Germans.

'What did you tell her?'

139

'That my father was killed in the war and you worked here. I didn't mention the stranger if that's what you're thinking. Remember — it's our secret.'

'You're a good girl.' Nefeli smiled.

'There's one other thing. When I left school, Konstantinos called me into the shop. He gave me some sweets again.'

At the mention of him, Nefeli felt a wave of despondency come over her. 'Did he say anything?'

'He told me to bring Agamemnon next time. He has something for you — a present — and as you've agreed not to see each other until the marriage, he didn't want to bring it himself. He said you would like it.'

Nefeli wondered what it could be and was thankful he hadn't taken it upon himself to call by the house himself.

'Fine, you can take Agamemnon tomorrow. Now help me put the remaining food in the pannier and we'll go home.'

*

Nefeli held her breath as they approached the house. The door was closed but she had no idea what she'd find when she entered. Maybe the man had gone, or worse still, maybe he was lying in wait ready to kill them, but she doubted that. Georgia waited at the end of the terrace until her mother entered and then gave her the all clear. When Nefeli pushed the door open, she was stunned to find the stranger sitting on the divan, surrounded by reels of cotton bobbins, sewing the trousers he'd been wearing since his arrival. She stopped to catch her breath. Such a scene of domesticity was the last thing she expected to find.

Heindorf held them out to show her and started to speak in German. 'They were torn...' His words brought her down to earth with a thud and she cut him short.

'I told you — no German!' she said angrily.

'*Signome,*' he replied, this time in Greek. 'I'm sorry. They were torn and I was trying to help.'

Nefeli marched across the room, ripped the trousers out of his hands and flung them across the room where they landed on the loom. Georgia, cowering in the doorway, was told to collect the cotton bobbins and put them back in the box and put them where they belonged, on top of the sewing machine next to the loom. The beautiful walnut box inlaid with mother of pearl, lined with velvet, and finished with lacquer, had once belonged to her grandmother and was given to her as a gift by her grandfather who had fought in the Balkan wars. He never returned, and the box remained a treasured memory. It was unthinkable that the man had been poking around in it. *What else had he been looking at while alone?*

Heindorf continued to sit on the divan without uttering a word. He'd tried to repair the trousers as a token of thanks. *Why was she so upset?* His eyes followed her every move and she in turn was aware of his gaze. He wanted to tell her to calm down but thought better of it. She was like a tigress, ready to pounce at any moment. Every now and again, her dark eyes threw him a glance: eyes that sparkled with intensity. How unlike Emmy this strange creature was — volatile, feisty, and proud — her very presence filling the room with an intense passion unlike any woman he'd ever known before. All the women he'd known had refined manners to the point of being restrained. This woman was a firebrand.

While Georgia tended the animals, making sure they were fed and secured in the outhouse for the night, Nefeli prepared their evening meal — leftovers from the taverna. She set the table for three and told him to join them. They ate their meal in silence, the tension palpable. After the meal, Heindorf bid them goodnight: he would retire to bed to leave the two of them alone.

'He seems a lot better,' Georgia said in a whisper. 'Can't we let him go now?'

Nefeli had already been mulling it over in her mind. 'I think tomorrow night is as good as any. I'll take him to the cove after midnight and in the morning he can try and attract the attention of a patrol boat.'

'What if none pass by?'

'Hardly a day goes by without a patrol boat on the lookout for *andartes* or some other unfortunate soul they can catch — like a fisherman without a license. You know what they're like.'

Her mother's words put Georgia at ease. It had been a long day and she was tired. Knowing that the stranger would be soon out of their lives, she curled up on the divan and soon fell asleep with the cat purring near her feet. Nefeli, on the other hand, was too consumed with a myriad of thoughts to go to sleep. She cleared the table and, after checking the stranger was fast asleep, reached for a glass of Konstantinos' raki, and went to sit outside on the terrace as she often did when she needed to think things over. The stifling heat of the day had been replaced by a soft breeze from the north. Too many questions swirled through her mind. What was the gift Konstantinos was sending her? *He'd asked Georgia to take Agamemnon so it must be something bigger than a box or candy or flowers.* Then there was Georgia's new teacher.

What business did she have poking her nose into their lives? She made a mental note to ask about her. Collaborators came in all guises and she might be one of them.

Nefeli drank her raki in no time. Konstantinos was right; it was a particularly good one. She closed her eyes, breathing in the sweet fragrance of the jasmine that covered the terrace with its mass of starry white flowers. The scent was always stronger in the evening — heady and sensual. Every now and again, she caught a whiff of pine resin from a cluster of trees at the top of the hill. It was at moments like this that she felt a surge of joy, despite the war stealing their souls and dulling their senses. Here she was, as free as a bird in a house surrounded by nothing but nature, and she had Yianni to thank for that.

Her thoughts soon returned to the stranger –Martin Tristan Werner Heindorf. *What a long name!* He had recovered quicker than she thought, so maybe it would be better for him to leave tomorrow night: one less headache for her. She would take him to Aphrodite's Cove after midnight, leave him there, and in the morning, he could lie in wait until the German patrol boats passed by and attract their attention. Then he would be out of their lives forever and she could face God knowing she had done right by another human being.

The combination of sitting on the terrace, soaking in the beauty of the night combined with two larger than normal glasses of raki, did wonders to still the turmoil in her mind and she decided to take a shower. In the warmer months, both she and Georgia washed outside in a small washbasin kept next to the tap at the side of the house. Nearby, hanging from a nail in a tree, was a larger tin bath, barely big enough to sit in but which was suitable to take a bath on hot nights such as this. Tonight, she was in the mood to do just that.

She placed the lantern on a rock, took down the bath and filled it with containers of cool water, and undressed. A chorus of cicadas filled the night air. What a delight to feel the water drench her hair and trickle down her body. Washing her hair and body with a block of olive oil soap, she felt alive and refreshed. It would be impossible to do this in Chora and it would be a luxury she would miss. Thoroughly refreshed, she towel-dried her hair and wrapped a larger towel around her body while humming a little tune to herself. She was not aware that she was being watched.

Heindorf, his senses already heightened, awoke to hear the soft splashing of water outside the house and quietly drew himself up to take a look out the window to see what was going on. His eyes focused on Nefeli's naked body only metres away and in that fleeting moment, watching her graceful movements and the voluptuous curves of her body, he forgot his pain. She was as beautiful as anything he had ever seen in his life. His heart pounded as it had never done in his life before. *My God, what a creature!* At one point she stood up and bent over to pick up a towel, the curves of her buttocks and breasts, glistening in the flickering lantern light. He slipped back into the bed, afraid she might realise he had seen her, but sleep did not come easy that night: his head was spinning and his body filled with visceral emotions that made him ashamed of himself. He realised he wanted her more than any woman he had ever wanted before in his life.

Chapter 17

IN THE MORNING, Nefeli set the breakfast table and called Heindorf to eat with them. He refused, saying he'd had a bad night and wasn't hungry.

'As you like,' Nefeli said, matter-of-factly, and returned to the table to eat with Georgia.

'What's wrong with him?' Georgia asked in a whisper.

Nefeli shrugged. 'He says he's not hungry.' She didn't want to talk about him any longer. Tomorrow he would be gone and everything would be back to normal: just the two of them.

After breakfast she attached the panniers to Agamemnon and waved Georgia goodbye, watching her wind her way up the hillside towards Chora. She was intrigued to know what Konstantinos had got for her. Returning to the house, she pulled back the kilims and told Heindorf he must get up. She needed to speak with him.

'Tonight you must leave. After midnight: I will take you to the cove myself.' She pointed in the direction of the sea. 'In the morning, a German patrol boat will pass. Wave it down. It will take you to Kos.' To make sure he fully understood, she tore a page out of the notebook and drew a primitive picture of a boat with a swastika and the shape of an island behind it. 'Kos,' she said, marking the island with an X. To emphasise the point, she also wrote 24:00 hours.

He nodded. *'Katalaveno.* I understand.'

'Good.' Nefeli got up to leave.

'Pou pas?' he asked in Greek. 'Where are you going?'

'Work.' She pointed to the paintings of the dolphins on the wall. 'The Blue Dolphin taverna — *my* taverna.' She tapped her chest proudly.

'Arbeit?'

Nefeli had no idea what that word meant. Heindorf suppressed a smile. Her gestures were expansive and demonstrative, her dark eyes flashing as she waved her arms in the air. She pointed to the food left out on the table and told him to eat it to get strong.

'For Kos!' she said.

'Katalaveno,' he said again. This time he smiled and his blue eyes twinkled, cheekily.

Nefeli turned away sharply, avoiding his gaze. She picked up Yianni's trousers, still draped across the loom, and handed them to him along with the Damascene sewing box. 'I'm sorry I was so rude last night. Your sewing is excellent. Please finish it.'

He noticed her hands were shaking and felt a lump rise in his throat. *How could he cause someone like her such distress? She didn't deserve it.*

'Is there anything else you need before I leave?' she asked.

'Yes.' Heindorf ran his hand over the stubble on his face. 'Can I shave this off?'

Nefeli looked through a box where she kept some of Yianni's belongings and found a tin that still contained his razor, a brush and comb, and two tins of cream which had long dried into hard unusable blocks. She threw the tins of cream away and placed the razor by the sink along with a small block of soap.

The day at the taverna passed without incident. One German patrol boat passed but didn't stop, and there wasn't a single customer all day. The solitude gave her too much time to think. Things were getting harder for her, but it wasn't that which bothered her: she had an uneasy feeling in the pit of her stomach. Something was about to go wrong and she had no idea what it was.

Konstantinos' gift turned out to be something quite unexpected — a wind-up gramophone and a box of records. Nefeli wondered if he'd bought it especially for her but it turned out to be nothing of the kind. He'd bought it for his first wife, Cassandra, and put it away after she died.

'No use for it here,' he said to Georgia as he loaded it onto Agamemnon's back. 'Your mother might as well have it.'

Georgia wasn't too sure. 'My mother may not appreciate another woman's gift,' she said, annoyed at his lack of consideration.

Konstantinos waved his hand in the air. 'Nonsense! I know your mother loved to dance. I've seen her at the village *Panigiria*. I don't suppose you have much music in the house since your father left.'

At the mention of her father, Georgia felt an immense sadness. *Was this thoughtless man really going to be her new father?* After tying the gramophone securely, he added that it was a token of his good intentions. Georgia noticed he omitted to say the word love.

At first Nefeli was pleased when she saw what it was, but her smile quickly faded when she learned it had belonged to Cassandra.

'Who does he think I am?' Her voice was filled with scorn. 'Second-hand goods for a second-hand woman!'

'I'm not sure he meant it that way,' Georgia replied, seeing the hurt on her mother's face. 'I'm sure his intentions were good.'

'Stupid man!' Nefeli said, angrily. 'You can take it back tomorrow. I never should have agreed to this marriage. I'll send a note and tell him I will go to see him.'

Georgia was alarmed. 'Mama, you can't do that. He will lose face.'

'If he is that thoughtless now, what will he be like later?'

Georgia knew there was no point talking about it any longer. By tomorrow, her mother would see things in a new light, but at the back of her mind she was pleased her mother was reconsidering the marriage.

Heindorf was surprised when they returned and he saw the huge brass horn of the gramophone glinting in the late afternoon sun. The look on Nefeli's face told him she was not happy. Soon he would be gone and he didn't want those last remaining hours to be filled with tension. He offered to help them bring it inside but Nefeli refused, saying it could stay on the terrace as she had no use for it. Dinner that evening was leftovers from the day before, but no-one was in the mood to talk and the tension was unbearable. In an effort to lighten the sombre atmosphere, Heindorf showed her the trousers he'd been sewing. Nefeli took a good look and smiled.

'Very good. In fact it's excellent.' She wondered where he learnt to sew like that.

She also noticed how handsome he looked after shaving. Realising she was blushing, she lowered her gaze, embarrassed at herself, but it was too late: Heindorf had noticed.

'Would you like a drink,' she asked, 'before you leave?'

'That's very kind.'

She poured a glass of raki for them both and then raised her glass. 'Here's to a safe journey.'

Heindorf smiled. 'Kos –ah yes!'

They sipped the raki in silence while Georgia played with the cat, letting it chase a ball on a string through the kitchen. The raki did wonders to relieve the tension.

'It's excellent,' Heindorf said.

'From Turkey — a very good one.' Nefeli picked up the bottle and without asking, poured him another.

'The gramophone,' he jerked his head towards the terrace, 'let's play a record.'

Nefeli protested. 'No!'

'Music is good, Nefeli.'

She stared at him for a few seconds. He had called her Nefeli. How good it sounded coming from his lips. She recalled the stolen kisses and averted her gaze. Georgia stopped playing with the cat, watching her mother's reaction.

'Music is good,' he repeated, and without waiting for her consent, went outside to take a better look at the gramophone. He wasn't sure if she even knew how to use it and offered to show her.

She gave a heavy sigh. 'Alright, but not here: inside.' She asked Georgia to help him while she cleared the table.

149

He showed her how to operate it and Georgia chose a record. The first one she pulled out of the box was called *Moon Over Athens*, a jaunty tango with a hint of gypsy soul about it. He attached a stylus into the small box on the curved tone arm and wound up the soundbox with the handle. Georgia watched him carefully, counting how many turns he made. The record gave a slight crackle but played beautifully. Everyone was delighted. Georgia danced round the room with her doll and they all clapped when the record finished.

'Let's play another one,' she said. 'This time you choose, Mama.'

Nefeli looked through the pile and pulled out a hit by the Babari Trio called *Love is an Eye*. This time she and Georgia danced while Heindorf watched. It was the first time he'd seen either of them happy.

'That's enough!' Nefeli said to Georgia when the record finished. She smoothed her flushed cheeks with her hands and tucked a few loose strands of hair back under her red kerchief. 'Time to go to bed, *agape mou*, or you won't be able to get up for school.'

She prepared her a bedtime drink of milk and honey while Georgia reluctantly prepared to sleep on the divan.

'Thank you,' Georgia said to Heindorf, as she covered herself with a light cotton sheet. 'That was great fun.'

Nefeli could tell that in her excitement, Georgia had forgotten Heindorf was to leave, and she didn't mention it. She kissed her on the forehead and turned down the light in one of the lanterns. The room was shrouded in a soft warm glow and the happiness of the evening was replaced by a frosty silence again. When Nefeli was sure Georgia was fast asleep, she told Heindorf he should prepare to leave.

'But first I must give you something.' She picked up one of the lanterns and went outside to the outhouse.

When she returned, she handed him his boots — the only item of clothing she hadn't destroyed — along with his few belongings which she'd kept wrapped in the cloth for safe-keeping. She watched his face and saw the look of surprise when he saw what she'd saved — his gun, knife, watch, and the wallet. 'I don't know why I kept them,' she said, more to herself than him. 'It was a dangerous thing to do.'

She couldn't help noticing the look of disappointment on his face when he opened the wallet. Whatever photographs he'd had were destroyed by the water.

'I'm sorry. Was one of them your wife?'

He nodded. 'Yes.'

'What is her name?'

'Emmy.'

'Do you have any children?'

'Yes, a daughter. Her name is Hannelore. She's about the same age as Georgia. I haven't heard from them in a long time.'

Nefeli felt a genuine sadness for him and hoped for his sake, they'd survived the heavy bombings he'd heard about that took place on a nightly basis all over Germany.

'And you, Nefeli? Your husband — what is his name?'

'Yianni: he's dead — 1941.'

Heindorf apologised. 'This damn war — we all suffer.'

Nefeli looked uncomfortable and changed the subject. 'Would you like another raki before you leave?'

'That would be wonderful, but only on one condition.'

'What's that?'

'That you have one last dance with me before I leave.'

Nefeli knitted her eyebrows together in a frown. 'Georgia...'

He didn't let her finish. 'She's fast asleep and I don't have much time. Please — just one dance.'

It was a quarter to midnight. Nefeli mulled it over. *What harm can one more dance do?*

'Alright; you win.'

Heindorf's smile broke into a broad grin. 'You choose the record.'

Nefeli leafed through the records and handed him one called *Esme*, a 1939 oriental Tango by Nitsa Molly. When the music started, Nefeli started to sway a little in rhythm with the music as she sat on the chair. Georgia stirred but quickly fell back asleep.

He stood in front of her and with typical Germanic formality, clicked his heels together and politely offered his hand.

'Would you dance with me, Kyria Nefeli, before I go?'

Nefeli stopped swaying and looked at him. His question startled her, as did the polite, gentlemanly manner in which he said it. *Oh what the heck! He will be gone in a few more minutes.* She took his hand and together they moved into the centre of the room. He held her in his arms and they began to dance. She was acutely aware of the pressure of his hand on the small of her back as they moved in time to the rhythm.

'Relax,' he said in a soft voice. 'Let the music take you where it will.'

It was obvious that he was a good dancer even though he was still unwell, and she followed his lead. He made her feel at ease and little by little, step by step, they became accustomed to the way each other moved. For Nefeli, it was like turning back the clock. With each step, she started to enjoy herself. Such a small thing, yet she realised how much she missed this sort of thing. In no time at all, her body flowed with the music, the room spun, and her skirt billowed with each twirl. When her kerchief slipped off, she didn't even bother to pick it up. She was like a small bird that had just learned to fly. Such was the exhilaration.

All too soon the music stopped and she pulled away, embarrassed by her actions. Heindorf thanked her and then said he'd best get going.

Nefeli felt flustered and awkward again. 'Yes. You are right. I will walk you to the beach.'

He gathered his few belongings and together they set off for Aphrodite's Cove. The lantern bobbed from side to side as she led the way, every step as sure-footed as a mountain goat. In no time at all, they reached the rocks. In the daytime they were easy to navigate, but at night they became dangerous, tussocks of seagrass masking dark crevices that made it easy to slip and break a leg. Nefeli brought the lantern closer, reached out for his hand, and guided him safely down to the beach. The cove was bathed with a soft diffused glow and the water glistened in the darkness from the myriad of stars twinkling like diamonds in the clear night sky. The sea was calm and the waves lapped gently and rhythmically at the water's edge, unfurling into thin slivers of soft white foam. There was something magical and peaceful about it, a beautiful place hidden away from the rest of the world and all its troubles.

'That's where I found you,' Nefeli said, pointing to a large rock. 'It must have been a strong wave to carry you that far. The lifeboat was over there — smashed to pieces.'

There was an awkward silence for a few minutes. Nefeli told him to stay hidden behind the rocks and when it was light, keep his eyes open for the German patrol boats. She reached out to shake his hand.

'Good luck.'

'I owe you my life,' he replied.

In that moment, as they shook hands, their eyes connected. Beyond her smile and shyness, Heindorf saw a deep emotion. He felt it too. Something quite beautiful that neither wanted to let go of. Nefeli pulled her hand away and turned to leave but he caught her arm and pulled her back. She spun around, like a rag doll falling into his arms. He held her close, whispering to her in German. 'I can't let you go, Nefeli. I've fallen in love with you.'

Her heart was pounding. She didn't understand the words but his eyes and actions said it all. His mouth covered hers, devouring her with such passion that she thought she would faint. She knew now what she'd known in her heart from the very moment she saw him naked on the kilim: that she wanted him more than anything she'd ever wanted in her life — even more than Yianni. It wasn't just his body: it was far deeper than that — something inexplicable. At the time, she'd tried to push those feelings away, but now, wrapped in his arms and intoxicated by his closeness, those feelings surged to the surface once again. What excited her too was that the feeling was reciprocated. He wanted her just as much. Both were attracted to each other like moths to a flame. It was electrifying, unbearable, unthinkable, and much worse than that — it was dangerous.

They lay in each other's arms on the seashore for what seemed like hours, kissing each other with an intensity that was electrifying. The urge to make love was overwhelming, but conscious of his broken ribs, they didn't consummate their love. Instead, they luxuriated in discovering each other's bodies in other ways, abandoning themselves to each other's caresses as their hands and mouths explored one another's bodies. Passion is good, Yianni used to tell her. It was he who taught her to be free, yet now, lying on the smooth sand still warm from the sun's rays, his familiar face that she had held so dear in her memory, was slowly fading — a kindly spirit who had watched over her until she was ready to let go.

After a while Heindorf asked her what she wanted. 'I can leave as planned — or I can stay. It's up to you?'

'You should get away from here as soon as possible. I want you to stay, but it's dangerous.' She kissed him and rolled over on the sand looking at the stars. 'I must get back. I can't leave Georgia alone for too long.'

He stood up and held out a hand to pull her up. She shook her hair from side to side, trying to get rid of the sand, pulled down her skirt, and picked up the lantern. Hand in hand, they made their way back to the house, occasionally stopping to kiss each other like young lovers. When they reached the terrace, he asked her to wait while he plucked a few sprigs of jasmine, inhaled its fragrance and tucked it gently into the centre of her blouse at the part which exposed her cleavage.

'The scent is as intoxicating as you,' he said with a smile.

Inside the house, Georgia was fast asleep, blissfully unaware of the events that had taken place.

'You had better sleep back in there,' Nefeli said, gesturing to the marital bed behind the kilim.

In the quiet of the night, she sat down on the chair, listening to him take off his clothes and get into bed. Her eyes focused on the gramophone as she thought about what had just taken place. *What had she done?* That question was far too difficult to answer now. Time would sort things out. She undressed, and feeling more contented than she had in years, slipped under the sheet next to Georgia and put a protective arm around her. *Please try and understand my sweetheart.*

Chapter 18

IN THE MORNING, Georgia asked her mother about the gramophone.

'Leave it for a couple of days. I will take it back myself.'

Georgia was relieved she wouldn't have to bear the brunt of Konstantinos' disappointment and asked if her mother still intended to call the marriage off. Nefeli told her they would discuss it another time; she was still thinking it over.

'Come straight back here after school,' Nefeli said as Georgia packed up her books and a small package of bread and cheese. 'I'm not going to the taverna today.'

When she was sure Georgia had gone, she bolted the door, took off her clothes and slipped under the covers in the marital bed with Heindorf. He was wide awake.

'*Guten Morgen mein Schatz.*'

'*Kalimera*... Martin.' For a brief moment, Nefeli found it strange to utter his name in such a familiar way, but now he no longer seemed a stranger to her. She planted a kiss on his lips. 'Did you sleep well?'

Martin gave her a broad smile. She loved the way his blue eyes flashed cheekily. 'The best sleep since I came here.'

Nefeli stroked his chest and buried her head in his arms. 'The pain — how is today?'

'I'm getting stronger by the day.' He commented on the beautiful necklace she wore — a blue glass dolphin attached to a gold chain. It nestled in her cleavage, glinting in the morning light that came through the window. He'd noticed she was never without it.

Her hand slowly moved from his chest, downwards towards his groin, and at the same time his hands reached for her head and gently pulled her to him, kissing every inch of her face and neck. 'Is this something you really want?' he asked, his voice serious, yet tender.

She threw him a coy smile. 'I am sure.'

That morning they consummated their love, savouring every moment of their time together. There was no going back. Even Yianni had not made her feel this way.

When Georgia returned from school, she was both surprised and confused to find Martin chopping vegetables while her mother fried pieces of fish. Not only that, but the table was laid with an embroidered tablecloth and in the centre was a ceramic jug filled with jasmine. As a rule, they ate off the old wooden table, once a deep cobalt but which was now a weathered pale blue covered with pot burns and knife incisions from years of cutting vegetables and filleting fish. Today, however, even the meal was served differently — on plates usually reserved for formal occasions. She looked at her mother quizzically, and saw her cheeks were rosy and her eyes shone. *Was it her imagination or was her mother actually happy again?* Georgia's young eyes absorbed it all.

The evening passed much as it had the night before and Martin suggested they play some more music. Georgia was delighted and looked anxiously at her mother for approval.

'Alright: just a few records and then it's time for bed.'

They played the same ones as before but this time added some more. Martin sat at the table watching while Georgia danced with her mother. Both were laughing and twirling in each other's arms. Every time the record finished, Martin clapped, shouting *bravo, bravo*. He loved the way such a simple thing like this brought them joy. Music was something he had taken for granted back in Germany. He couldn't recall Emmy swirling round the room with Hannelore. She was far too gracious. Georgia was thrilled when he showed her how to work the gramophone.

'What a pity it has to go back,' she said, winding the handle, 'just when we are having fun.'

'It doesn't belong to you?' Martin asked, surprised.

Nefeli scooped her long hair back from her face, looping it in a loose knot at the nape of neck. 'I'm afraid not. It was a gift — one I can't accept. It's a long story,' she added with a sigh.

'It's from a man in the village who wants to marry Mama.' Georgia blurted it out before Nefeli could say anything.

Seeing her mother's reaction, Georgia's face reddened: she had spoken out of turn. The smile on Martin's face disappeared and the atmosphere quickly turned sour. The music finished, the laughter faded, and Nefeli told Georgia it was time for bed. Martin took this as a cue to retire for the evening. He went outside to wash himself and when he returned, Georgia was

159

already in bed. Barely able to look Nefeli in the face, he bid them both goodnight.

In the morning, Nefeli was outside feeding the hens when Georgia appeared. Her face was downcast.

'Did I say something wrong last night, Mama?'

Nefeli put down the container of food and wiped her hands on her apron. 'No, but I've decided once and for all, I cannot marry Konstantinos. I will take the gramophone back myself tomorrow and tell him.'

'What should I do if he calls me after school and asks if you like it?'

'Avoid him at all costs. Make an excuse: you have to get home to do chores for me. Under no circumstance say anything to anyone. Now go and eat your breakfast, you're late already.'

Georgia turned on her heels and ran back to the house. 'Damn!' Nefeli said, under her breath. She was not looking forward to confronting him, but it had to be done, and the sooner the better.

Georgia ate her breakfast alone and then prepared her books for school. Martin was still asleep and her mother busied herself in the outhouse hiding his belongings again. It was far too dangerous to keep them in the house.

'Will you go to the Blue Dolphin today?' Georgia asked as she was leaving.

'Yes.' Nefeli's response was cool and unemotional, yet at that moment, she felt anything but unemotional. 'Meet me there as usual.'

Martin had deliberately stayed in bed until Georgia left. He'd hoped Nefeli might come to him as she did before, but that was not to be. When he heard the clatter of a tin and the outside tap running, he looked outside the window and saw her filling water bottles for the animals. She was deliberately avoiding him. After checking there was no-one else around, he went outside and confronted her. She was in the outhouse, feeding Agamemnon.

'I'm sorry if I upset you last night. It was really none of my business.'

Nefeli hadn't heard his footsteps and she accidentally knocked a water bottle over when she stepped back in fright.

'Look what you made me do!' she said angrily. Unable to contain her emotions any longer, she sat on an upturned box and buried her head in her hands, sobbing. 'No, no. It's me who should be sorry,' she said, wiping her tears away with her skirt. She looked up at him. 'We have to talk, but not here. Go back to the house.'

Nefeli finished her chores and composed herself. When she returned to the house, there was a surprise in store for her. Martin had prepared breakfast — fried eggs — and served it up as elegantly as possible with a centrepiece of fresh jasmine. He pulled the chair out for her and it took her all her time not to burst out crying again. It had been such a long time since someone had treated her this way.

'Eat — before it gets cold,' he said, breaking off a chunk of bread and dipping it into his eggs with gusto.

After they'd eaten, Nefeli started to clear away the plates, but Martin put out his arm and told her to stay where she was. He made her a Greek coffee and brought it to the table. It made her smile.

'Good. I am glad you are smiling again,' he said. He watched her take the first sip. '*Kalo einai?*'

She smiled again. '*Kalo*. Where did you learn to make this?

'On Crete. Our cook taught me.'

Nefeli knew he was waiting for her to explain the situation on both their minds. 'It happened just before you came here. The matchmakers wanted me to get married again.'

Martin hadn't heard the word "matchmakers" and he checked in the dictionary to see what it meant. *Kupplerinnen*! His eyes widened as he tried to take it all in. These Greeks with their old-fashioned ways puzzled him.

'We were fine until the terrible storm when I lost some of my close friends.' She omitted to tell him some were *andartes* and blew up the German boat. 'They used to help me — give me fish every day in return for me cooking them a meal. Now I have no-one and life has become very hard. I have Georgia to think of so in the end I accepted their proposal.'

He reached across the table for her hand. 'Come away with me, Nefeli. Leave this island.'

She pulled her hand away and looked him straight in the eyes. 'And go where?'

'Germany. This war will be over soon. The Allies are gaining ground.'

'I don't speak German.' She burst out laughing. 'Besides, you are married! Have you forgotten that?'

'Nefeli, don't you realise — I've fallen in love with you. I can't live without you.' His outburst startled her. 'I will ask Emmy for a divorce and then we will be married. I'll take care of you. You will have a good life in Germany — Georgia too. I will love her like my own.'

'*Agape mou*, how could I live with myself knowing I had stolen another woman's husband? God would not look kindly on us.'

Martin felt this was an argument he could not win. He could already tell by the icons in the house that Nefeli was a believer. 'After what I've seen, I no longer believe in God,' he said. He didn't want to burden her by telling her the things he'd done in the name of the Third Reich.

'God brought us together.'

'No, Nefeli! Fate brought us together.'

She crossed herself. 'Don't speak like that. We will be cursed.'

He got up, pulled her up from the chair and gave her a long and passionate kiss. Wrapped in his arms, she clung to him, wishing their problems would go away.

'We will go to Kos and from there to Rhodes where I am stationed.' His eyes pleaded with her. 'And when the war finishes, we'll go to Germany. Please say yes: I know you have the same feelings for me.' He put his hands firmly on her shoulders. 'I want to ask you something, and if your answer is yes, I will say no more. This man — the one you said you will marry — do you love him?'

Nefeli shook her head. 'Of course not!'

'Then don't do it. I beg you.'

'You don't understand our ways. It's not that simple. I gave him my word, but loving you has put an end to that. I've decided not to go ahead with the marriage because I know now that I could never have the same feelings for him that I have for you.'

Martin felt a sense of relief but it was short-lived.

'When I tell him this,' Nefeli said, barely able to utter the words, 'I will have dishonoured him — and his family. On this island, honour means everything.' She lowered her gaze, fighting back the tears. 'It won't be easy for me.'

163

'Which means you will be free to leave with me. I've already told you I will protect you both.'

Nefeli pulled away. 'I need time to think.'

Martin was becoming exasperated. 'We don't have time, my darling.'

Nefeli knew he was right but her head was spinning and she couldn't think clearly. 'Let's talk about it later. I want to go to the taverna today. If anyone notices it's been closed for two days, they might come knocking on my door. Neither of us wants that.'

It was hard for her to leave him, but she needed time alone to think things over and the coastal walk to the Blue Dolphin helped clear her mind. At lunchtime a boatful of fishermen from a nearby island called by and left her some fish in exchange for her cooking them *kakavia*.

A German patrol boat also stopped to check everyone's ID and conduct their usual search of the premises. This time it was a different translator and the men were more civil. She gave them each a glass of *Vysinada* that she'd made herself from sour cherries, and one of them even left her a few drachmas. Sometime later, Georgia arrived and Nefeli's first question was about Konstantinos.

'He called me over after school but I said I was in a hurry — like you said.'

'And the teacher — is she still asking questions?'

'No. She just gives us exercises while she reads all day. I don't think she's a real teacher at all. Some of the other children don't even turn up now. I will be glad when our teacher gets back.'

Nefeli thought it was now time to involve Georgia in her thoughts. She might be young, but life had forced her to grow up quickly. 'Let's go and sit on the sand for a while. I want to talk to you,' she said.

They took off their shoes and headed to a spot near the water's edge.

'You know we have a special bond, *Georgaki mou.*' Georgia wondered where this was heading. 'And we share a special secret.'

'Yes, Mama; what is it you're trying to say?'

Nefeli wasn't quite sure how to phrase it. Playing with the truth wasn't good with Georgia. She was bright and observant.

'Well, I've been having a talk with Martin.'

'Martin!' Georgia blurted out. 'Is that what you call him now?' She was angry and upset.

'My darling, he has a name so let's be civil shall we? I've been talking with him about his... situation.'

'You mean that he could be killed at any moment if the islanders knew he was here — and us too.'

'From what I gather, he has a few broken ribs but he is recovering well. In a few days he will leave.'

Georgia gave a sigh of relief. 'How?'

'He will go to Aphrodite's Cove after dark and will wait there until a German patrol boat passes in the morning. Then he'll try and attract their attention. It shouldn't be too hard as they keep a lookout for anything suspicious along the coast.'

Georgia was stunned. In her small world, it sounded too good to be true. 'When does he plan to leave? You told me before he would leave but he's still here.'

'Maybe in three days' time, four at the most.' Nefeli hoped it would be longer but for the moment, this would put Georgia's mind at rest. 'You remember the nice German man who gave me the fish the other day? Well, he said not all Germans were bad. I'd say he was a good one, wouldn't you?' Georgia screwed her face up but Nefeli took no notice and continued. 'And you know what? I think Martin is one of those good Germans too. He hasn't attempted to rob or kill us, has he? He's had plenty of chances — and he was kind enough to show us how the gramophone worked.' As an afterthought, Nefeli added that they'd had fun dancing to the music.

Georgia got up and walked to the water's edge enjoying the feel of the soft foaming waves unfurling around her ankles. *Maybe her mother was right about him. At least plans were in place for him to leave at last.*

The fact that Nefeli had only told her daughter half the story did not bother her at that moment. Acceptance was a gradual thing.

*

Another evening passed in peace and harmony. After a dinner of fish soup, Nefeli decided to do some weaving. It had been a while now since she'd touched the blanket she was working on. Georgia sat at the table doing her homework and Martin asked her about Alexander the Great. Nefeli threw the shuttle from side to side, listening to them talking. She smiled to herself knowing that he was making an effort to win her over.

There was no music that night: just the sounds of the cicadas and the clack, clack, clack of the loom shafts lifting up and down each time Nefeli pressed her foot on the foot paddle. It was late when they retired to bed and Nefeli was exhausted. The events of the last few days were catching up on her and she needed a good night's sleep. Martin would have to wait until the morning to find out what her answer was.

Chapter 19

IT WAS STILL dark when Nefeli left the house and in the twenty minutes it took her to reach the small, whitewashed church of Panagia Thalassini, a diffuse morning light had already painted the rocky landscape a rose-tinted glow. The grass was damp with dew and the smell of sage and thyme filled the air. At this time of the day, the bright cobalt church dome appeared subdued but in a few hours, the early morning magic would be gone and the harsh summer sun would once again be beating down and the colours blindingly intense.

The church stood perched on a rocky outcrop at the southern tip of the island and was surrounded by a paved area of polygonal stones with an outer wall where the villagers would sit and talk after a service. Several majestic cypress trees stood on either side the entrance, and at the back of the church, where the land dropped down to the sea, a cluster of pines had taken root, sheltering the church from strong winds that battered the island during storms.

Nefeli pushed open the heavy wooden door, stepped inside and made the sign of the cross. The interior was cool and sparse with very little decor except for a simple altar covered with a gold embroidered cloth on which stood three icons, and a stand filled with sand for candles. Yet in this simplicity, there was a holiness she found comforting. The fragrance of incense, which had seeped into the stones over the years, was heavy and soothing. She lit a candle and placed it among the icons and knelt to say a prayer. One of the icons was of special significance. It was said to have been snatched from the clutches of a giant octopus by a fisherman near the rocks below during a storm. For that reason, the church was built to house the icon in this breathtakingly beautiful spot on the promontory and named in her memory — Our Lady of the Sea. It was also known to work miracles and was the reason for Nefeli's visit. She kissed it, said a prayer, and asked for a blessing.

She had come here often after learning of Yianni's death and felt God had comforted her. Now she was looking for something divine to help her again: a sign, however small, that would shine a light on her predicament. The candle flickered and crackled in the silence of the room and after ten minutes of prayer, she felt her heart lighten. When she left the church, a white dove flew past her and hit the wall near the door. Stunned, it fell to the ground by her feet flapping its wings awkwardly. She bent down to pick it up but it managed to evade her grasp, making a few awkward little jumps backwards until it eventually flew away into the pine trees. She looked up at the sky and saw an eagle circling gracefully on the look-out for its prey. After a while, it flew out to sea. Nefeli took this to be a sign. The dove was safe: Martin would be safe. *Her prayers had been answered. God had listened after all.*

On the way back to the house, Nefeli heard the soft tinkling of bells in the distance and wondered if Georgia had let the goats out. Then she noticed several goats which didn't belong to her. She was surprised; no-one ever grazed their herd in this area. Moments later, Mikis the goatherd appeared, clambering over the rocks, calling and whistling to them. It was unusual to see him on this part of the island. Knowing that she had declined his marriage proposal, she wanted to hide, but there was nowhere to go. He saw her, and waved. She waved back and hurried on. Within minutes, both the goats and Mikis had disappeared. It all happened so fast, she almost thought she'd imagined it, but it gave her a nasty feeling to see him so close to the house. She must warn Martin to be extra vigilant.

Georgia and Martin were eating breakfast when she returned. Georgia asked where she'd been.

'For a walk to the church of Panagia Thalassini and on the way back, I saw Mikis the goatherd. It was only for a few minutes, but I want you to take care.' She directed her gaze to Martin. 'We cannot let our guard down.'

Nefeli told Georgia she would be going to Chora today and they would return together. She would be waiting outside the school.

'Will you return the gramophone?' Georgia asked.

Nefeli nodded. Martin saw this and felt a surge of optimism. He knew that when Georgia left, she would give him the good news. He didn't have to wait long. As soon as they were alone, he pulled her into his arms and kissed her.

'My love, I couldn't sleep. Tell me, what have you decided? Will you come away with me or...?' He couldn't bear to think there might be another decision. They sat down on the divan and he held her hand. 'Don't keep me in suspense any longer.'

She stroked the back of his hand with her fingertips. 'You have stolen my heart,' she began. She felt the tension in his hand as he tightened his grip in anticipation. 'But I have decided that...' She struggled to find the right words.

'That you don't love me enough! You still see me as the enemy.'

'No! You've got it wrong. I *do* love you, but I can't leave, because it wouldn't be right.'

He let go of her hand and wrapped his arms around her. She loved it when he did that, yet at the same time, she hated the way she melted in his embrace. She needed to be strong.

'I don't care if you're the enemy. One day this war will be over and our countries will be friends again. I may be young and unworldly, but I know that will happen. That's life. The problem is I cannot leave with a married man. It wouldn't be right. I could never forgive myself for breaking up a marriage and in the end it would be a burden that would poison our perfect love. That would be unbearable.'

Nefeli looked into his eyes. They were filled with love but she could see the pain he was going through. She too felt that same pain.

'I have thought long and hard about this,' she continued, 'and the last thing I want is for my heart to rule my head.' She felt a lump rising in her throat. 'I've decided that you must leave alone. When this war is over, go back to Germany and if you still have the same feelings for me, then divorce Emmy and I will come to you, but I cannot live in sin.' Martin opened his mouth to protest. Nefeli put her finger on his lips. 'Enough. We must be

171

strong and do what's right. I can wait — six months, a year, two years, however long it takes: for the rest of my life if I have to.'

'I love you more than life itself,' he replied. 'I know I will never love like this again and so I am prepared to wait — as long as you never stop loving me.'

Nefeli cupped his face in her hands and kissed him. He looked like a wounded animal. 'Never,' she replied. 'You will fill my dreams at night. That will sustain me.'

She stood up and smoothed down her skirt, trying to hide the tears welling up in her eyes. 'Now please excuse me; I have to go to Chora and take back the gramophone.'

'This man in the village...'

Nefeli gave him a quick kiss. 'Enough! He is nothing.'

He watched her get ready, fixing up her hair at the back with silver pins and donning an emerald green kerchief edged with a gold trim that matched the trim on the sleeves of her white cotton blouse. She would turn heads; he knew that, and felt a pang of jealousy thinking what would go through the minds of these people with their strange and unfamiliar attitudes. She fetched Agamemnon and he helped her load the gramophone and box of records on his back.

'Remember to keep the door locked,' she said, and kissed him goodbye.

Chapter 20

NEFELI HAD BEEN so busy with her problems she'd forgotten it was market day in Chora. The square was filled with stalls laden with whatever produce the islanders could lay their hands on from dried fish, pulses, to honey, vegetables and herbs. On the far side people were also selling goats, sheep, chickens, and caged singing birds. Thankfully, the intoxicating fragrance of the watermelons and golden melons combined with the herbs sweetened the air from the animal dung.

She guided Agamemnon around the stalls hoping that people would ignore her, but the gramophone attracted unwanted attention and people started to call out: *Hey, Kyria Stellakis, are we going to have a dance.* She ignored them and headed for *O Ermis.* Konstantinos was inside chatting to a customer when he saw her arrive and tether Agamemnon to a nearby mulberry tree. When he saw the gramophone, he stopped his conversation mid-sentence. His face paled.

The customer asked if he was alright but he quickly pulled himself together. 'Yes, yes, it's nothing.'

He ushered the woman out of the shop just as Nefeli walked in. It was Kyria Thekla, another busybody and Nefeli knew it would soon be common knowledge in the village that the Stellakis woman who ran the Blue Dolphin had paid a visit to Konstantinos — with a gramophone.

'I need to speak with you — alone,' Nefeli said to him after Kyria Thekla had gone.

Konstantinos put the closed sign on the door and asked her to take a seat at the table reserved for his clients who called in for a drink.

'What is it, Nefeli? Have I offended you by giving you a gift?'

Nefeli didn't want to mention the fact that it belonged to Cassandra: that wasn't what she'd come to say. 'Not at all; in fact it was a generous thought.'

'Then why have you brought it back?'

Nefeli could barely look him in the eyes. 'I'm afraid I have something to tell you.'

Konstantinos smiled. 'Do you want to bring the wedding forward. Is that it? If it is, I'm sure we can arrange something. That would be wonderful.'

'It's not that. I'm sorry to disappoint you, but I've decided to call the wedding off.'

His face dropped. 'Why? I thought it was what you wanted. I thought...'

'Konstantinos, it wouldn't be right. I don't love you.'

His face had a look of disbelief. With those few words, she had pierced his heart like a dagger.

Nefeli felt terrible and wanted to reach out to ease his suffering, but her hands remained clasped together in her lap. She couldn't bear to touch him. What a mistake she'd made agreeing to such a foolish proposal in the first place.

'I'm sorry,' she repeated again.

Konstantinos pleaded with her to reconsider. 'You will learn to love me.' There was desperation in his voice and he put his hand out to touch her, but she moved away swiftly. Her response was like a slap in the face. 'How will you survive alone? Is it that you don't want to live here in Chora, because if it is…?'

'No. It's nothing of the sort. I realized I am happy as I am. I am not alone; I have Georgia. The war will be over one day and things will return to normal. I told you, I don't love you. You will find someone else. Forget me — please.'

To Nefeli's surprise, he started to sob. 'I have always loved you, Nefeli, even when you were married to Yianni. Could you never see that? Cassandra was second best to you.'

This revelation only made Nefeli feel worse. She got up to leave. 'Please help me with the gramophone and I will bother you no more.'

He wiped his eyes and went outside to help her. They had only been together a short time but already a small crowd of busybodies were starting to gather outside. Ignoring them, he carried the gramophone inside while Nefeli carried the box of records.

'I'm really sorry,' Nefeli said, this time looking him in the eyes. 'Truly, I am. You're a good man and I never meant to hurt you, but it was not meant to be.' With that, she turned and left.

Konstantinos watched the crowd stand aside as Nefeli took Agamemnon's reins and departed. He left the closed sign on the door and went to the back of the store to drown his sorrows in a bottle of raki.

175

Nefeli was deaf to the comments the villagers were making, but it was evident they knew something was wrong. '*Po po!*' someone said. 'Not even married yet and they've already started to argue!' Another laughed and called him a silly old fool for choosing such a haughty woman as a bride.

It was only right that Nefeli tell Kyria Eleni about her decision and she headed straight there. Already there were two or three women on her doorstep including Kyria Thekla.

'*Kalimera*, Kyria Eleni, could I have a word with you please?'

Kyria Eleni ushered her inside and closed the door. 'I heard you returned Konstantinos' gift. Is that right?'

Nefeli was hardly surprised to hear she knew about it. News travelled fast in Chora.

'Have you had a disagreement already?'

'I cannot marry him. I don't love him.' She blurted the words out nervously. 'It was a mistake.'

Kyria Eleni crossed herself. '*Aman!* A mistake!'

Nefeli looked at the ground. 'Yes, a grave mistake. I shouldn't have agreed to all this.'

Kyria Eleni looked at her as if she had lost her mind. 'You silly woman: don't you recognize a good thing when you see one! Where will you get a man like him again? You are not a young girl anymore, you know.'

'I am happy as I am.'

Kyria Eleni scoffed. A few minutes passed before either spoke. Nefeli knew it was no use arguing her point and Kyria Eleni was too upset to speak. She saw her commission disappear in a flash. Worse still, her reputation as a matchmaker would be ruined.

'And what am I going to say to his poor mother? She will berate me for shaming the family,' Kyria Eleni said, angrily.

Nefeli was sick and tired of listening to her. She put her hands over her ears to block out the old woman's words. 'I was not marrying his mother — I was marrying Konstantinos. It's *his* feelings I am worried about,' she shouted out, 'not his mother's.'

'*Aman*! What ingratitude! They told me you were a wild one, but I never expected this.'

It took Nefeli all her time not to lose her temper and she got up to leave. 'I came to offer my sincere apologies for putting you all through all this, but you must understand, it's for the best. Thank you for trying to help me. I appreciate it — and please convey my apologies to Kyria Vervatis.'

There was nothing more to be said and Nefeli left. The two women who had been on the doorstop earlier had moved away and were standing further down the street wondering what was going on. Nefeli led Agamemnon to the school, passing Konstantinos' store on the way. It was still locked and she felt a terrible pang of guilt knowing that he had taken this so badly. When she reached the school, she called the teacher aside and told her she had come for Georgia. Georgia's face dropped when she saw her mother. She was an hour early; something had gone wrong. The teacher asked if everything was alright and Nefeli told her Georgia was needed at home. She would make sure she was back in class tomorrow.

'What's wrong, Mama?' Georgia asked when they were alone.

'Let's get away from here as soon as possible.'

The further away they got from the village, the more Nefeli

relaxed but she refused to talk about it. Dragging Georgia into all this wasn't a good idea.

Martin had been on tenterhooks the moment Nefeli left the house and he could tell by the look on her face that it hadn't gone well. A cloud of gloom settled over them again and in a house where privacy was non-existent, both Nefeli and Martin were forced to wait until Georgia had gone to sleep before they could talk. Even then, they couldn't talk openly and Nefeli suggested they go for a walk to Aphrodite's Cove.

As soon as they were a fair way from the house, they fell into a passionate embrace. It was at moments like this that they shut the world out. They reached the cove and lay down on the sand just as they had the night Heindorf was supposed to leave. Already aroused in each other's company, they lost all inhibitions, making love that set their bodies on fire even more. Every moment was precious. When it was over, Nefeli felt an intense mixture of joy and relief. Joy that such a love existed, and relief that she'd called off the marriage to Konstantinos. It took a while before the subject was broached.

Martin was reluctant to bring up the subject of her meeting in Chora, fearing Nefeli might retreat into herself and crush the beautiful moment, but in the end, it was Nefeli herself who spoke first.

'I told him,' she said. 'He didn't take it too well. He told me he loved me and I felt sad for him. He's a good man.'

Martin felt a pang of guilt at putting her through such an ordeal, but they loved each other and soon he would take her away from all this.

Nefeli propped herself on her elbow and looked at him.

It was hard to imagine she'd once hoped he'd die. 'That chapter of my life is closed. We must not sully our last few days by talking about it any longer. She traced a line from his chest to his abdomen with her index finger. 'My future is with you now.'

He pulled her on top of him, the small glass dolphin on the gold chain hung over her breasts as she leaned over him, glinting in the moonlight. She took out her silver hairpins and let her black hair tumble over him. She was so beautiful: every inch of her body oozed strength and sexuality, yet there was also a fragility that made him want to protect her.

'You drive me crazy,' he whispered, nibbling her ear.

She laughed: the first real laugh in a long time. Until Martin, Nefeli hadn't realised how much she'd suppressed her emotions. Now this stranger — who was no longer a stranger — had breathed life into her again and for that she would love him forever. She stood up and walked to the water's edge dipping her toes into the soft white foam.

'It's beautiful. The water's still warm.' She kicked the foam into the air playfully.

Martin sat up watching her as she went deeper and deeper into the sea, splashing the water over her body. She reminded him of a playful dolphin; the ones he'd seen many times in Greek waters. She was a free spirit and he loved her for it. *My little gypsy, so strange yet so familiar: how did I ever find you?*

After a few minutes, she returned to the beach. 'Come on, get up. There's something I want to show you.' She threw his clothes at him. 'I want to show you my taverna — the Blue Dolphin.'

'Are you sure it's safe?'

'Quite sure; no one ventures out at this time of night these days, and certainly not as far as the taverna.'

There was almost a full moon which made it easier to follow the dirt path without using the lantern and alerting any German night patrol boats, and it wasn't long before the angular shape of the taverna came into view. Perched on the edge of the rocks overlooking the water, it looked a desolate place at night and Martin didn't like the idea of her being all alone in such an isolated spot.

'It's no more isolated than the house,' Nefeli said with a smile, but Martin didn't seem convinced. 'Besides, I never stay open in the evenings. What's the point when there are curfews and no-one has any money to spend? If people want to go out, they will go to a *kafeneio* in Chora or Mikrolimano.'

She looked for the spare key hidden under a barrel near the outdoor oven and as soon as they were inside, lit the lantern.

Martin looked around at the wooden tables and rush-bottomed chairs and nodded in approval. 'A place like this should be filled with life.'

'It was before the war. Now hardly anyone comes here: a few sponge divers from Kalymnos, fishermen, and the locals when they feel like a change.' She told him that she relied on the charity of friends to bring fish in exchange for a meal but since losing a couple of close friends in the storm, fish was harder to come by. 'So as you see, I spend less time here now.' He picked her up and sat her on a table. She saw him flinch when the pain from his broken ribs tore through his chest, and chastised him. 'You shouldn't do that? I am far too heavy.'

'I want to take you away from all this. It's a hard life and you deserve better.' He unbuttoned her blouse and started to caress her firm breasts. 'Is this why you wear this necklace?' He held the small blue glass dolphin in his fingers. 'Because of here.'

Nefeli nodded. 'A gypsy came here one day selling all sorts of trinkets — before the war. She had lots of amulets, bracelets and necklaces. Most were evil eye charms, like those over there.' She pointed to a couple of blue glass eyes hanging on the wall. 'I chose this because of the taverna, because being here has made me happy.' She sighed. 'At least it did once.' Then she lightened up. 'I wanted to show you this before you left, so that you can imagine what I am doing when you are in Germany, and in turn, I shall remember we were here together: it will keep me going until we meet again.'

Martin loved the fact that something so simple made her happy, but it saddened him to think she still refused to leave with him.

She slid off the table and took the key to the gate in the cave off the wall. 'Come on, there's something else I want to show you before we go back.'

When they stepped back outside, a soft sea breeze was blowing, tempering the intense heat of the day, and the scent of the sea filled their nostrils. They retraced their footsteps back along the dirt track, veering off at the point in the rocks where the cave was hidden from view. Heindorf got a shock when he saw the cave.

'No-one would ever know it was here,' he said in surprise. 'And the iron gate — who put this up?'

'At the time Yianni built the taverna, he kept his boat in a nearby cove, but when he left to fight the Italians, he knew

I wouldn't use the boat and decided to keep it here so that it wouldn't get stolen. He constructed this gate to keep any would-be thieves out. It's said that the cave was used years ago by pirates and Greeks fighting the Turks.'

Nefeli omitted to tell him the *andartes* used it to store arms. She was already taking a risk in taking him there, but the weapons were safely hidden away. There was also another reason she took him there.

She lifted the lantern high so that he could see the Blue Dolphin caique. 'The night the storm brought you to the island, water spilled in over the rocks and pushed it further inside. It's not damaged though.' She turned to face him. 'The reason I am showing it to you is that should anything go wrong and you are not able to alert one of your German patrol boats, I want you to take it.'

Martin looked at her and took her hand. She was shaking. 'You said the patrol boats passed every day.'

'That's true. It's just in case...'

'In case of what — is there something you're not telling me?'

'No. I am hiding nothing. I am simply offering it to you in case...' Nefeli couldn't finish the sentence. Since leaving Chora, she'd had an uneasy feeling in the pit of her stomach but Martin's love and their intimacy had pushed it to the back of her mind. She had wanted him to see the taverna before he left, but something there had sparked a fear in her. He'd sat her on the same table where the matchmakers had first broached the subject of a marriage proposal and it was now beginning to sink in that everyone would turn against her. In her heart, she knew they only had a day or so left together. She tried to push it to the back of her mind.

'Come on. Let's get back. We've been away from the house too long as it is.' She held the lantern while Martin closed the gate and then started towards the rocks.

He called out to her. 'Nefeli: haven't you forgotten something?'

She turned. 'What is it?'

'You forgot to lock the gate.'

'That's okay,' she replied. 'No-one ever comes here anyway.'

Chapter 21

WHEN GEORGIA WALKED through the town to the school, she found it unusually quiet. The square was empty and the *kafeneia* closed. As she passed through the square the church bells began to toll. For a moment she thought she'd got the days muddled up and it was Sunday. She pushed the school door open and saw the teacher sitting at her desk reading a book, but there were no students.

The teacher snapped her book shut and called her over. 'Georgia. I have something to say to you.' Georgia wondered if she'd done something wrong or even worse, if the Germans had been to the village and either shot someone or taken more people away. 'I think you should go back home straightaway,' she said in a solemn voice.

Georgia couldn't believe what she was hearing. 'Why?' she asked, with a mixture of innocence and curiosity. 'Have I done something wrong? Was my homework not good enough?'

The teacher put her hand out to stop her questions. 'No Georgia. You are a good student. I didn't want to be the one to tell you, but something terrible has happened.'

'Were the Germans here again?'

'It has nothing to do with the Germans. It's the owner of *O Ermis, o* Kyrios Vervatis: he's dead.'

Georgia's face paled. *Konstantinos — dead!* She stared at the teacher as if in a dream. 'Did he have an accident?'

The teacher shook her head. 'I'm afraid he hanged himself. His mother found him in the store early this morning.'

Georgia's eyes widened in disbelief and she burst out crying. She knew it had something to do with her mother's refusal to marry him. The way the teacher looked at her told her that she thought that too.

'Wipe your eyes, *koritsi mou*.' The teacher tried to comfort her, but Georgia's tears flowed like a river.

Konstantinos: the man who had given her sweets and a smile — the man who wanted to be a father to her — dead by his own hands. She simply couldn't get her eight-year-old head around it. She was sure everyone would blame her mother.

'So be a good girl and go straight home,' the teacher said. 'It's for the best — until things quieten down a little.' She walked Georgia to the door and checked the street. It was still empty and the bells were still tolling. She bent down and put her hand on Georgia's shoulder and in a low voice said it might be wise if her mother stayed away for a while too.

At these last words, Georgia felt as though she would burst out crying again. *So she was right: they did blame her mother.* She ran down the street as fast as her legs would carry her. Nothing would be the same again.

*

NEFELI WAS IN the marital bed with Martin when she heard the sound of someone running towards the house. No-one ever ran to the house. She looked through the window.

'It's Georgia,' she said, and jumped out of bed, clutching a sheet around her. 'Something's wrong: desperately wrong!' She threw Martin's clothes on the bed. 'Get dressed — quickly.'

Georgia burst through the door just as Nefeli parted the kilims, the sheet still wrapped around her body. If Georgia had suspicions about her mother's feelings for Martin, they were now confirmed. She threw her books on the floor and screamed at her before running back outside. 'It's all your fault. Now he's dead!'

Nefeli ran to the door calling her back. 'Georgia! Who's dead? Come back here.'

Georgia ignored her and ran towards the brow of the hill, disappearing into a stand of pine trees. Nefeli threw on some clothes and ran after her. When she got there, she found Georgia curled up in a foetal position on a bed of pine needles. She was sobbing uncontrollably and Nefeli pulled her into her arms.

'Agapi mou: what's happened? Who's dead?'

Georgia told her what had happened and that the teacher had advised them both to keep away from the village. Nefeli felt her blood run cold. She had been fearful that the villagers would turn against her, but never in her wildest dreams did she think Konstantinos would kill himself. She closed her eyes and rested her back against the trunk of a tree, trying to comprehend it all. She felt numb, staring into space, oblivious to the drone of the bees and the beauty of the dappled sunlight through the pines.

She lost all track of time as she sat in this state: maybe it was a few minutes, maybe longer. It was Georgia who brought her back down to earth. She was tugging at her skirt asking her what was going to happen, but Nefeli was so numb the words didn't even register.

'Mama!' Georgia screamed at her.

Nefeli blinked. 'I'm sorry, my darling. I didn't hear you.'

'What are we going to do?' Georgia asked.

There was little Nefeli could do: the damage was done. Her thoughts turned to Martin. He had to get away. She couldn't risk him being on the island a moment longer. This was now uppermost in her mind. She pulled herself together, brushed away the pine needles from her clothes, and hurried back to the house with Georgia trying to keep up with her.

Martin was pacing the room, nervously. 'What's happened?' he asked.

Nefeli asked Georgia to feed the animals while they talked. Georgia threw Martin a dirty look as she walked away.

Nefeli slumped down on the divan. 'You have to leave — tonight.' He sat next to her, holding her trembling hands as she told him what happened. 'Konstantinos — the man I was to marry — is dead. He hanged himself.' She could barely say the words. 'Georgia doesn't know the details, but the fact that the teacher sent her home and told us both to stay away for a while means they blame me.'

Martin squeezed her hands tightly. 'My darling, this is terrible news, but you are not to blame. You did what you thought was right.'

Nefeli shook her head and gave him a sad smile. 'I told you that you didn't understand our ways.'

Once again, he pleaded with her to leave the island, but she remained steadfast. 'Let's not go over this again. We have to plan your escape immediately.' A few minutes of silence passed between them as the reality sunk in that they only had a few more hours together. 'You must go to Aphrodite's Cove tonight around midnight and wait for the patrol boat as planned.'

Martin held her in his arms, stroking her long silky hair. He could feel her body shaking as she sobbed and knew he must be strong for her. Eventually Nefeli tore herself from him and went to the outhouse to get his things. Georgia was there feeding Agamemnon. It was evident her mother had been crying. Nefeli removed a few stones from under the hay and retrieved Martin's few belongings.

'You did all this because of him, didn't you?' Georgia said. 'You should have left him to die.'

Nefeli looked at her daughter's sad eyes. 'He's leaving tonight.' She paused for a moment. 'One day you will understand.'

Back at the house she handed Martin his things. 'There's something else I want you to take.' She reached for the German/ Greek dictionary. 'When you get to Kos, look for this man, Christos Grivas. He translates for the Germans at the port. Give him his dictionary back and tell him to give me a sign that you arrived and are safe.' She gave him an old leather satchel to carry everything in.

Georgia returned and, for the rest of the day, hardly anyone spoke. The atmosphere was highly charged. Georgia would not breathe easily again until the stranger — or Martin, as her mother now called him — had left the island, and Nefeli and Martin were too depressed knowing that with each minute that ticked by, their love affair was drawing to a close. Nefeli tried to pass the time by weaving on her loom but she couldn't concentrate and made mistakes. By the time the sun started to set, she was overcome with light-headedness and felt faint. It was impossible to carry on. Martin gave her a glass of water and Nefeli's hand caressed his fingers as she took it from him: a small but important gesture. Every touch, every glance, was magnified. *Martin my love. How will I carry on without you?* Her eyes said it all.

In the midst of this heartache, Nefeli remembered that the goats had not been let out to pasture and asked Georgia if she'd take them out for an hour or so. She cautioned her not to go too far away from the house. As soon as she'd gone, Nefeli and Martin fell into a passionate embrace, smothering each other with kisses and breathing in each other's scent one last time.

Chapter 22

NEFELI HAD KNOWN her refusal to marry Konstantinos would be frowned upon, but she could not possibly have known what would transpire after she left Chora. The news that she had called the marriage off reached Kyria Vervatis' ear even before she'd left the village. Someone knocked on her door to tell her that Nefeli had gone to see her son with a gramophone. Kyria Vervatis already knew of the gift and had chastised her son at the time for giving Cassandra's prized possession away. She'd always had a soft spot for her daughter-in-law, a subservient and shy woman who was also intensely religious. Because of this, Kyria Vervatis was able to dominate Cassandra, even if it meant going against her husband's wishes. Nefeli on the other hand, was a spirited woman, but Konstantinos said he wanted her and so she calculated it would be better for him to have a wife than remain a widower. In her eyes, her son wasn't getting any younger and he needed to have children of his own to carry on the family name and business. Nefeli would provide the heir the Vervatis family had longed for. Now their dream was shattered.

The ungrateful Nefeli had blackened the family name. The fact that Nefeli and Konstantinos weren't even married yet was beside the point; the matriarch of the family had embraced her and she had embarrassed them.

There followed a hasty meeting between Kyries Eleni, Angeliki, and Kalliope, and after a lengthy discussion, Kyria Eleni thought it might be a good idea to see if they could salvage the marriage. Maybe Nefeli had cold feet for a good reason, but it was worth checking out. At the back of their minds was their own reputation as matchmakers. Everyone agreed, but first they needed to talk with Konstantinos. By all accounts, *O Ermis* remained closed and he refused to answer the door to anyone.

By the time the women reached the store, a small crowd had gathered outside. The shutter was down and people were peering into the window to see what was going on. The crowd parted when they saw Kyria Vervatis arrive. She banged on the door and shouted for her son to open up, but there was no answer. In the end she went back home to fetch a spare key. When she returned, she asked the crowd to go away and leave her son in peace. Sensing her plight, they moved away, some of them going to the *kafeneia* to discuss the situation, even though it was none of their business.

Kyria Vervatis found her son sitting at the table at the back of the store drinking raki and listening to a record. She admonished him for his melancholia, telling him to pull himself together. 'All is not lost, my son. Kyria Eleni will pay Nefeli a visit. She has been on her own a long time: maybe she had last minute nerves.'

'I wish that was so. I love her, but the look in her eyes told me she didn't love me. It's over.'

There was a knock on the door and the man who owned one of the *kafeneia* in the square poked his head around the door.

'Kyria Vervatis, can I have a word with you?'

In a whisper, he told her that when Mikis the goatherd heard what took place, he made a comment that maybe she didn't want him because she had someone else. Kyria Vervatis looked stunned. Surely that was not possible.

'He said he'd seen her twice after dark — once near the house and another time near Aphrodite's Cove — and each time she was in the company of a stranger,' the *kafeneio* owner said.

'I thought he never grazed his goats on that side of the island.'

'These days he's ventured further afield because the long hot summer has made grazing difficult. The earth is parched.'

'Who is this man?'

'He had no idea. He didn't get close enough to see him but, by all accounts, widow Nefeli seemed happy in his company.' He winked mischievously as if she knew what he meant.

Kyria Vervatis narrowed her eyes. 'Maybe he's making it up. After all, she did turn him down.'

The *kafeneio* owner shrugged. 'That may be so, but I doubt it: he's not clever enough to make up such a story. He's a simple man.'

'Ask him to meet me at my home straightaway,' said Kyria Vervatis. 'I will hear what he has to say.'

The man left and Kyria Vervatis returned to her son who was getting more depressed by the minute, took the needle off the gramophone, and smashed the record on the floor.

'Pull yourself together,' she shouted angrily. 'You are a Vervatis! We are a proud family. Now put that bottle away and get back to your business. You must put on a brave face.'

With that, she left him to face his sorrows alone.

Mikis the goatherd stood in the dining room clutching his cap in his hand. He was not used to being in such a house and felt uncomfortable. The Vervatis were one of the richest families on the island and Kyria Vervatis kept a comfortable home with all the accoutrements to match her standing: fine furniture, a multitude of textiles including rugs, and walls filled with photographs, paintings, and icons. It stood in stark contrast to his own stone house with its dirt floor and no such luxuries.

Kyria Vervatis covered her nose with her fine handkerchief, trying to block out the odour of animals which filled the room due to his dirty clothes. Trying not to keep him any longer than absolutely necessary, she didn't ask him to sit down and neither did she offer him a polite drink.

'What have you got to tell me?' she asked, matter-of-factly. 'What did you see at Kyria Stellakis' house?'

'It was quite dark, you understand — and I wasn't that close to the house.'

'Yes, yes. Get on with it. Did you see her with another man?'

Mikis started to stammer out of embarrassment. He should have kept quiet; now the villagers were looking towards him for answers. 'I did, but... but...'

'My dear man, please get to the point. What were they doing?'

'The first time I saw them they were walking towards the cove. I didn't think anything of it except that it was unusual to see her out so late. I thought maybe she had a relative over from another island. Then I saw her again and this time I followed her. They went to Aphrodite's Cove.' Mikis' face was turning red with shame.

Kyria Vervatis fixed her eyes on him. 'What were they doing?'

Mikis could barely say the words. 'They were playing around.'

'What do you mean — playing around?'

'You know — what people do when they like each other.'

Kyria Vervatis sighed heavily. In her eyes, there was no doubt Mikis was a halfwit, but she also knew he was trying to protect her from something she didn't want to hear — Nefeli was playing around with another man.

Her face reddened with anger. 'Thank you. That will be all. You may see yourself out.' She gave him a few drachmas for his trouble.

Mikis bowed graciously, mumbling apologies for having eyes that had seen something bad. He told her that God would strike him down for being an interfering busybody who had brought suffering to them all. Kyria Vervatis waved him away dismissively. To learn of Nefeli's affair from a simpleton cut deeply. It made them look even bigger fools.

Later that evening, Kyries Eleni, Angeliki, and Kalliope were summoned to the Vervatis household to discuss the situation. Konstantinos, still drunk from too much raki, refused to believe Mikis' story. For him, Nefeli was too honourable a woman to do such a thing and he considered his words to be the ravings of a spurned man. After much discussion, even the three matchmakers couldn't think who it could be and they were sure that if there was another man in Nefeli's life, Dimitri and Toula would have known about it and said something. They went through every available male on the island — even the married men — and the more they talked, the more they believed Mikis was imagining things. It might even have been Georgia who was out with her mother. The matter was left as discussed earlier: Kyria Eleni would pay Nefeli a visit.

Unfortunately the disastrous event that unfolded the next day changed everything. When Kyria Vervatis went to wake her son up in the morning, she found him gone and, thinking he had gone to the store early, thought no more about it until news reached her that *O Ermis* was still closed long after it was due to open. When his neighbours saw there were no rush-bottomed chairs, brooms and baskets, birdcages and spades, and other paraphernalia spilling out on the footpath as normal, they knew something was seriously wrong.

Kyria Vervatis arrived in a foul mood and unlocked the door, ready to chastise her son again for acting like a love-struck fool, but when she saw his body hanging from the ceiling in the semi-darkness, she collapsed in a faint. By the look of the empty raki bottles, Konstantinos had been drinking heavily. It was also evident that he had been playing more records. In a state of despair, he hanged himself with the belt of his trousers and kicked away the chair. His body was still warm and there were wet marks on the table where the raki had been splashed. From this, it was deduced that it had only just happened.

The men cut down the body and laid him on the long counter while the women tried to revive Kyria Vervatis. In his clenched hand was a note.

My dearest Nefeli whom I loved from the depths of my heart. I made my bed for two and you did not want to share it. You were not mine, but for a short time your sweet smile gave me such joy that sometimes I thought I would go mad. Try not to think of me as a coward for my heart is scarred, my senses numb, and

my eyes no longer see. Please light a candle for me and say a
prayer in the Panagia Thalassini. Bless you, Konstantinos.

When the note was read out, the room went quiet. 'Aman,'
someone said after a while. 'What a curse to be struck with the
sickness that is love.'

Everyone agreed.

Later that evening, surrounded by close friends who had
come to pay their respects, the grieving Kyria Vervatis told
them she wanted to catch the perfidious Nefeli in the act. She
intended to pay her a surprise visit and she wanted to do it that
night. Everyone agreed.

Chapter 23

GEORGIA TOOK THE lantern and led the goats towards a large section of scrubland just above the olive grove and sat under a tree while they grazed. The soothing tinkling sound of their bells helped her keep track of them but they never strayed too far. She brought her knees up and rested her chin on them and with one finger, drew a pattern in the dirt thinking about what had taken place. All she could think about was that her world had collapsed around her because of the stranger. She hated him because he was the enemy and blamed her mother because his presence had clouded her mind. If only she'd left him on the beach to die. Without water he would have died within a day.

After more than an hour she was so tired she could barely keep her eyes open and decided to head back home. She stood on a rock and called out to the goats. At that moment, she saw twinkling lights in the distance. She rubbed her eyes, thinking it was her imagination playing tricks on her. When she looked again there were more, coming over the brow of a hill just over a kilometre away in the direction of Chora. In that fleeting moment she realised exactly what it was: the villagers were heading towards the house, carrying lanterns.

She emitted a sharp scream and ran as fast as she could back to the house.

'Mama! The villagers are coming,' she called out as she neared the house.

Nefeli jumped up from the divan and ran outside to take a look. In the distance she could just make out a cluster of tiny lights, flickering in the darkness like fireflies. Her blood ran cold. She ran back inside and told Martin he had to leave straightway. There was not a moment to spare. She picked up his bag and stood by the door, looking in the direction of the olive grove while he pulled his boots on.

Nefeli pulled Georgia aside. 'I must get Martin away from here before the villagers arrive. If they find him, they will kill him.' Georgia's eyes widened and she started to cry. Nefeli shook her. 'Listen to me. You must do as I say or...' She stopped mid-sentence, not wanting to frighten her more than necessary. 'Get into bed and pretend to be asleep — not here on the divan: in the marital bed where we used to sleep. Everything must look normal. When they arrive, they will ask where I am. You must say I probably went for a walk — that it's something I do when I can't sleep — got it? The other thing is, if they ask if a man has been here, say no.'

Georgia nodded. 'Where are you going? I'm scared.'

'If you do as I say, there's no need to be scared.' Nefeli gave her a kiss on the forehead. 'Now get into bed — quickly.'

Georgia ran into the darkness of the marital chamber, changed into her nightdress and clambered into bed. Her heart beating fast, she clasped the icon of the Virgin to her breast and said a prayer.

Nefeli and Martin set off towards Aphrodite's Cove. Carrying a lantern was out of the question as it would be seen by the villagers, but thankfully there was enough light from the full moon to see the track. The fact that they'd walked this way together before helped enormously. The problem arose when they neared Aphrodite's Cove. The pathway petered out into the blackness of the rock crevices. Nefeli went first, but when she turned round to offer him her hand, she froze. There were lights in the distance and they were not the lights they'd seen heading towards the house. These were heading straight towards them along the coastal path from the direction of the Panagia Thalassini.

She made the sign of the cross. '*Theé mou*: there's more than one group.' She looked at Martin. 'This means they are searching the coast: but why?'

'They must suspect something.'

'What is there to suspect?' Nefeli ran her hand through her hair in despair. 'We've been so careful.'

The lanterns were drawing closer and Nefeli was becoming more and more frantic. 'If you stay here they will find you. There's only one thing left to do. You must go to the cave and take the caique. The gate is unlocked.' She clung to him. '*Agape mou*, you must go on alone. I will stay here. If they see me, they won't bother you. It's your only hope.'

There was no time for a discussion. Martin knew she was right.

'The path is easy to navigate in the moonlight, but do you think you can find the cave?'

'I think so.' He squeezed her hand. 'I have a good memory.'

'And are you strong enough to drag the boat out and row? Your ribs haven't healed yet, you know.'

He fixed his eyes on her. 'I will do it, my darling. I will do it for us.' Nefeli fell into his arms, fighting back the tears. He turned her face to look at him. 'Let me look at you one last time.' He covered her mouth with his, tasting the sweetness of her lips. 'Forgive me, but I cannot say goodbye.'

'Nor I, but now we must part. Every second you stay here, your life is in danger.'

He turned to leave and she caught his arm. 'Wait a minute.' She took the glass dolphin from around her neck, kissed it and pressed it into his hand. 'To remember me by.' The pain in her heart was more than she could bear. 'My dearest, when you are in foreign lands, open your window at night and I will come to you in a dream.'

He took one last look at her face, as if committing it to memory, and walked away in the direction of the cave. Nefeli felt as if her legs would give way at any minute, yet somehow she found the strength to carry on. She wrapped her shawl around her shoulders and headed back, taking one last look in the direction of the coastal path. Martin had gone. It was as if it had all been a dream.

When she left the house it had been in semi-darkness with only one lantern burning in the kitchen for Georgia. Now it was surrounded by light: so much so that she could clearly see a mass of figures congregating around the building. She glanced over her shoulder and saw lights swarming near Aphrodite's Cove too. It didn't look good. All of a sudden, she heard Georgia's scream and ran towards the house, stumbling over pebbles and thorny bushes, and cutting her bare feet and grazing her legs in her haste.

Someone saw her and called out. 'There she is!'

All eyes were peeled on the shadow emerging out of the darkness. Georgia forced her way through the throng and ran into her mother's arms.

'They want to kill you, Mama,' she screamed.

Nefeli clutched her daughter to her. 'Did you mention Martin?' Nefeli asked.

'No. They asked me about a man and I said I hadn't seen one, but they don't believe me.'

As Nefeli neared the terrace, she saw at least twenty villagers, armed with sticks, glaring at her. In the centre was Kyria Vervatis.

'The whore has returned,' Kyria Vervatis said. The chorus of onlookers joined in, hurling abuse.

'Be gone, Kyria Vervatis. Leave us in peace,' Nefeli said sharply. 'What is done is done. I cannot bring back your son.'

Kyria Vervatis scoffed. 'Listen to her! The wretch has the devil in her.' She walked up to her, holding her face close to Nefeli's. 'Let me look into the eyes of the devil.'

A terrified Georgia clutched her mother tightly.

'Please go away, I am begging you. You're frightening my child.'

'There's gossip about you.' Kyria Vervatis indicated to someone in the crowd and they pushed Mikis the goatherd forward. 'Go on — tell them,' she said, waving her arm towards the people. 'Tell them what you saw.'

The blood drained from Nefeli's face.

Mikis dropped to the floor on his knees clasping his cap in his hands and begging Nefeli to forgive him. Someone poked him with a stick. 'Speak, you fool!'

He was filled with guilt at the torrent of hatred he'd unleashed and reluctantly said he'd seen her with a stranger and that on one occasion he'd seen them at Aphrodite's Cove.

'Go on: what were they doing?' Kyria Vervatis asked, clearly enjoying this.

Mikis began to stammer. After a vigorous kick in the back, he said she was cavorting with the stranger. When asked if it was sexual, he looked at Nefeli begging forgiveness.

'He's lying!' she shouted to the crowd. 'There is no man. If so, where is he?'

'We'll find him. He won't get away,' someone replied.

The look in the villagers' eyes was one of hatred. At that moment she caught a whiff of smoke in the night air. Terrified, she glanced in the direction of the Blue Dolphin and saw that the sky was red. They had set the taverna on fire.

Nefeli spun around to face them. 'Good God! What have you done?'

Kyria Vervatis looked at her malevolently. In her eyes, the widow was responsible for her son's death and she wanted retribution. The crowd started to close in on her as she tried to back away. Kyria Angeliki pulled Georgia from her grasp and held her tightly, holding her head in such a way that she wouldn't see what was about to take place. Georgia screamed and kicked and bit her, but to no avail. Kyria Angeliki was too strong.

'Stop them!' Nefeli screamed out to Kyria Eleni.

No one came to her defence and the crowd closed in more. All of a sudden, she felt a sharp pain in the small of her back and fell to the ground. Someone had hit her with a stick. The pain was so bad she started to feel nauseous and faint.

'Whore! Slut! Fallen woman!'

A woman lurched forward and spat at her. She recoiled in terror but there was nowhere to go. She was trapped. Then she felt another whack, this time on the back of her head — and another on the side of her face. Something cracked and the blood thudded through her body as she tried to crawl away, her hand reaching out for mercy. She made one last attempt to get up but her strength was fading, the faces began to blur and their voices turned into a cacophony of venomous shrieks. The sticks rained down on her and in that moment, death seemed a welcome release.

Amid the terrifying sounds she heard a gunshot. It was quickly followed by another, this time much closer. The sea of legs in front of her parted and she recognized Dimitri's voice ordering them to leave. Somewhere in that fog of semi-consciousness, she was aware of him threatening to shoot anyone who touched her. Someone spoke and Dimitri pointed his rifle at them saying he wouldn't be responsible for his actions if they didn't leave immediately. Georgia ran to her mother and pounded on her chest, begging her not to die. Dimitri bent down and pulled Nefeli into a sitting position, but she flopped like a rag doll back onto the floor. Toula was with him and rushed to cradle her friend, rocking her to and fro while Dimitri made sure the crowd dispersed.

'It's no longer safe to stay here,' he said to Georgia. 'We're taking you both to safety.'

He wrapped the bleeding and badly bruised Nefeli in a blanket

203

and carried her towards Aphrodite's Cove where his fishing boat was pulled up in the shallow water. Gently, he and Toula lowered Nefeli onto a soft bed of fishing nets and the three of them pushed the boat back out to sea. Enveloped in a combination of the gentle swell of the sea and the sound of lapping water against the boat, Nefeli slipped into unconsciousness.

Dimitri rowed the boat past the Blue Dolphin. The flames that had consumed the taverna had now died down and all that remained in the blackness of the night were the ruins of the walls and a smoke haze, rising gently towards the silver moon. The smell of smoke drifted out to sea, heavy and pungent, polluting the night air. Toula cradled the terrified and exhausted Georgia in her arms; careful not to let her see the ruins of the Blue Dolphin. Her gaze fell on Nefeli, her face now a swollen mass of cuts and bruises, and she looked at Dimitri in dismay. Neither could find the words to express the depth of their despair. What had taken place would haunt them for the rest of their days.

Chapter 24

THE SMALL EXCURSION boat pulled up alongside the jetty and, one by one, the tourists stepped off the boat, cameras at the ready. They headed towards the seafront with its half-a-dozen tavernas, *kafeneia,* and a general store selling everything from sponges and sea-shells, postcards, sunhats and sunscreen, to komboloia and blue-glass evil eye amulets. At the end of the jetty, the first person the group confronted was Stephanos sitting behind a table next to a large board advertising his donkey treks to the village of Chora. In a loud voice he called out that there were only eight donkeys left and if they didn't book now, they would have to walk. Immediately, a few congregated around him and booked their rides.

'Be back here in an hour,' he said, counting his takings, 'after you've eaten.'

A few people decided to have a bite to eat before their donkey ride, while others walked along the seafront to explore the nearby coves and partake in a spot of private sunbathing or snorkelling.

It was a perfect summer's day and the crystal blue water sparkled like a jewel in the sunshine. For the last two months the island had enjoyed a brusque business, but as a rule, most people flocked to the larger islands in the Dodecanese with their fancy resorts and packed beaches. The people who came here did so to escape, because, unlike many of the Aegean islands, this island was like stepping back in time. The ferries were infrequent; there were no hotels, and only a handful of rooms to rent. It was as if the inhabitants had purposely shut themselves off from the rest of the world.

Georgia was wiping the tables outside the Blue Dolphin taverna in readiness for the next customers when she spotted a woman with sun-bleached blonde hair tied back with a black ribbon, taking photographs of two fishermen mending their nets on the beach. She showed something to the fishermen, a few words ensued, and after some minutes, the men pointed in the direction of the tavernas. The woman turned around, took more photographs of the seafront, and moved away.

Georgia thought no more about it and went back inside to tend to her *kakavia*. It was her speciality, and today she had excelled herself and the rich broth was bursting with flavour. The addition of saffron combined with a good crop of tomatoes from her garden and the fact that she used seawater rather than plain water to cook the fish, took this simple fisherman's dish to another level. She had the radio on and was listening to *To Trehandiri*, Greece's entry that year in the Eurovision Song Contest, while washing a few glasses. She turned it up and started humming to the tune. At that moment, the blonde lady walked into the taverna and sat at a table near the window with a view of the beach. Georgia went over and asked if she'd like anything to eat or drink.

The woman saw the word *"Kakavia"* written on a large blackboard. 'That's fish soup isn't it?' she asked. She spoke English but Georgia could tell by her accent that she was German.

'Yes. We call it Fisherman's Soup and the dish is a speciality of the house. My mother used to make it.'

'I would like that, please.' She ordered a carafe of white wine to go with it.

Georgia placed the wine on the table along with a basket of crusty white bread and a small platter of *mezethes*. The woman commented on the music and asked what the song was about.

'It's a love ballad. A man is singing to his lover about a time they spent on a small boat called a *trehandiri*, and they are sailing around the Greek islands.'

'That's beautiful,' she replied.

She made some notes in a small diary and checked her camera while Georgia served another couple who arrived five minutes later. They acknowledged the German woman with a nod but did not sit with her. Georgia surmised that the woman was travelling alone.

When everyone was served, Georgia went behind the counter, observing the blonde lady from afar. She appeared to be of a similar age, tanned with deep blue eyes, and still quite beautiful despite the passing years. She had an aristocratic elegance and confidence that Georgia admired about certain German women, and she'd seen quite a few over the past few years since the island had become increasingly more popular with the tourists. The other couple finished their meal before her and left. They were taking the donkey trek to Chora. Ten minutes later, Stephanos passed the taverna leading the donkeys with the tourists on their backs. He waved at her as he passed by. The German woman took a photograph of them.

'You didn't want to join them?' Georgia asked.

The woman replied that she had other things she wanted to do. Georgia cleared her bowl and asked if she enjoyed the *kakavia*.

'Excellent. A memorable meal. Would you think me rude if I asked for the recipe? I would love to try it when I return to Germany.'

'I'm sorry. I can't share this recipe with anyone. It's a family secret.'

Georgia's response was swift and the woman apologised if she had offended her. To show she was not offended, Georgia brought her a slice of baklava. 'On the house,' she said with a smile.

'Do you mind if I ask you something?' the woman said.

'Not at all.'

She picked up her bag and took out an old black and white photograph and showed it to her. 'I'm trying to locate this place and the woman who is sitting on a nearby rock. The fishermen said they've only been here a few years but thought you might be able to help me.'

Georgia put on her glasses and peered at the image. In that moment she felt as though her legs would give way and pulled out a chair to sit down.

The woman looked startled. 'Are you alright? You've gone quite pale.'

'Where did you get this?' Georgia asked sharply.

'It was in my father's belongings. We found it after he died.' The woman was concerned. 'Are you sure you're alright. You look terrible — and your hand is shaking.'

Georgia put the photo on the table. 'This photo...' She could barely get the words out. 'It's my mother, and the building is this one — the Blue Dolphin — but the one in this photograph was burnt down.' She got up and went over to the counter to fetch a bottle of ouzo and two glasses. 'I need a strong drink. Perhaps you will join me.'

On hearing that the woman in the photo was the taverna owner's mother, the German woman slumped back in the chair, looked squarely into Georgia's eyes and after a long pause, let out a heavy sigh. 'You can't imagine how much I've searched. I came to Greece every summer for the past three years and all I had to go on was this photograph. No name — nothing. Now I've finally found it.'

When the magnitude of what the woman was saying sank in, Georgia asked who her father was.

'Martin Tristan Werner Heindorf.'

Georgia swallowed hard. *Martin! The same Martin her mother had loved — the reason they lost so much.*

'My father was in the Luftwaffe and was stationed here during the war. I was eight at the time and knew very little about his work. My mother used to tell me he was fighting for Hitler — nothing else. For a while we didn't hear from him. When the Germans surrendered in Greece in 1944, he was held as a prisoner of war and returned to Germany after the war ended.' The woman took a deep breath. She had a sad look in her eyes. 'My mother said that when he came back he'd changed — the war changed many people and few wanted to talk about what took place. I was too young at the time to notice, but as I grew older, I realised my parents' marriage wasn't a happy one but they stayed together until the end.

'My mother was the first to pass away — cancer. It wasn't a good death. During those last few days, I was with her every day, and I asked her why she and Papa stayed together in what was obviously an unhappy marriage. She said something that has haunted me ever since. "Do you know, my darling, I am sure your Papa met another woman when he was in Greece. He never talked about it, but I knew — a woman senses these things, you know". When I asked why she didn't confront him about her suspicions, her reply was that whatever happened during the war, she would forgive. She was just happy to have him home when so many of their friends and family had been killed. Besides, she loved him deeply, so merely having him there was enough for her.'

Georgia listened without uttering a word. Until now, the memory of Heindorf and the summer of '44 had stayed locked away in her mind. His name had never been mentioned again. It was as if he'd never existed — except for the ramifications his presence had brought to her life. Now, all these years later, those memories surfaced again and her mind was reeling.

The woman continued. 'After my mother died, I wanted to ask my father if there was any truth in what Mama had said, but I couldn't bring myself to do it. And then a year after her death, he surprised me by saying he was planning a holiday to Greece. He said he wanted to see the islands where he'd been stationed. He was so excited at the thought of it, that bringing up my mother's conversation — particularly about another woman — just didn't feel right.

'The day he was due to leave, I was putting his bags in the boot of the car in readiness to take him to the airport, when he took a bad turn — chest pains, nausea and light-headedness. He'd suffered from a heart condition for a while but because of the medication he took, we thought it was under control. I wanted to call the doctor but he protested, saying he would be fine and didn't want to miss his flight. Ten minutes later, he was dead.'

Georgia felt a lump rising in her throat and poured them both another drink.

'I have no brothers and sisters and called my aunt — my father's sister. Naturally, we were too distraught and occupied with the funeral to empty his suitcases at the time, but when we did, a week or so later, we found this.' She indicated to the photograph. 'There was also something else with it.'

She opened her bag again and pulled out something wrapped in tissue paper. Georgia stared at it and years of pent-up emotions threatened to get the better of her. Tears welled up in her eyes. It was her mother's necklace — the blue glass dolphin. All those years, she had thought her mother had lost it. Now she knew the truth. Her mother must have given him both the photo and the necklace the night he left. For years, Georgia had wondered if Martin made it off the island on that fateful night when the villagers turned against them. Now she knew he had, and was suddenly overcome by a strange mixture of conflicting emotions. At the time she had wished him dead. Now she was glad he survived.

'The necklace belonged to my mother — the woman in the

photograph. The original Blue Dolphin taverna was reduced to a shell during…' She didn't want to say the villagers burnt it down. It would seem an unlikely story to a foreigner anyway. 'There was an accident and it burnt down. Many years later, we rebuilt it and extended it further, which is why it looks different to the one in the photograph. I was going to rename it but the original was built by my father and it seemed only right to keep it in his honour.' Georgia looked closely at the photograph. 'My mother is sitting on that rock over there.' She pointed to a rock where she used to sit when watching Socrates mend his nets. 'The image of the Blue Dolphin sign that you see in this picture was painted by an itinerant painter who also painted the walls in my parent's home at the same time. It was painted on wood and as a consequence, didn't survive the fire which is why there is a new sign. It's no wonder no-one recognized it.'

Georgia smiled to herself when she thought about the time she spent with her mother during the war — until that fateful night. They were difficult years, yet the memories were good. Since the taverna re-opened, some twenty-five years earlier, her life had been one of uneventful peacefulness. The taverna only opened during the summer months, and even then it was fairly quiet. The rest of the year, she spent tending her garden, orchard, and olive grove, or visiting friends in Athens. What she had just learnt today rocked her to the core. She asked the woman's name.

'Hannelore: I live in Hamburg.'

'I can see how much all this has meant to you. You needed answers and I understand. In a way, you and I are not dissimilar. I needed answers too, and like you, I kept things hidden for as long as I care to remember.' She smiled. 'Fate has a way of bringing people together in the most unexpected of circumstances: wouldn't you agree?'

Hannelore commented favourably on the ouzo before continuing. Like Georgia, it gave her time to absorb the situation. 'If this woman is your mother, can you enlighten me? If something happened in Papa's life when he was in Greece, I need to know.'

Georgia nodded. 'We both do.' She looked at the time. 'There's someone I think you should meet. Your boat won't be leaving for another three hours.' She put the closed sign on the door. 'Come on. Let's go for a drive.'

Hannelore followed Georgia to the end of the street where her battered old car stood. They drove south along a coastal road. The new road followed the same path Georgia used with her mother years ago. Neither women spoke during the journey. Hannelore distracted herself by taking in the spectacular views of the Aegean — a shimmering turquoise blue in the afternoon sun — and the barren rocky landscape dotted here and there with whitewashed houses and the occasional small, blue-domed church.

Ten minutes later, they arrived at a newly whitewashed stone house surrounded by an orchard, olive grove, and a large vegetable garden. Under the shade of the jasmine and vivid red bougainvillea-covered terrace, two cats lay between pots of geraniums and basil, lazily soaking up the warmth of the sun. At the sound of the car, a large black and tan dog bounded out of the house, wagging its tail. Georgia stroked it playfully and at the same time indicated to Hannelore to follow her. The door was ajar and as they neared, they heard a voice call out. "Georgia, is that you?"

Georgia stepped inside. 'Yes, Mama, it's me, and you have a visitor.'

The old white-haired woman sitting at her loom stopped what she was doing and turned around. 'A visitor! We never have visitors. Who is it?'

Georgia asked Hannelore to come in. 'Mama, this lady has come all the way from Germany...' She paused to watch her mother's reaction. 'She came to find you.'

Nefeli reached for her glasses. 'Me? Who on earth would come all the way to see me?'

She put on her glasses and peered at Hannelore carefully. In that moment, Georgia was sure there was some sort of recognition. As for Hannelore, she had trouble equating the beautiful woman in the photograph with this frail, white-haired woman who was now so bent over she could barely move without the help of her daughter. What was most shocking of all was that the woman's face was badly disfigured down one side. Hannelore swallowed hard. Maybe she should have been like her mother and left well alone.

'Let's go outside and sit on the terrace,' Georgia said. 'And I will prepare coffee for us.'

Nefeli picked up her walking stick. Her steps were slow but steady, and with Georgia's help, she managed to walk outside into the bright sunshine. Georgia pulled up a cane chair, set it near the long wooden table and puffed up a cushion before helping her mother sit down. When she turned to go back inside, Nefeli caught her arm.

'No coffee: fetch a bottle of good wine — the one from Naoussa.'

Georgia and Hannelore looked at each other.

'Are you quite sure, Mama? You shouldn't be drinking you know.'

Nefeli waved her arm in the air. 'Bah! Do as I ask. It's not every day we get a visitor from Germany.'

When Georgia brought out the red wine, she saw that her mother was staring at the German woman with a strange expression. Hannelore looked uncomfortable.

'Mama, let me introduce you. This is…'

'I know who she is: she has his eyes,' Nefeli said, her words measured and soft. Hannelore and Georgia exchanged a quick and slightly uncomfortable glance. 'I remember them as if it was yesterday — such beautiful blue eyes.'

Georgia knew immediately who she was referring to. 'I know this has come as a shock and I deliberated over whether I should bring her here.'

'You did right,' Nefeli replied. She reached for Hannelore's hand and clasped it tightly. 'All these years I wondered if he made it back to Germany. Now I know.' She crossed herself and mumbled a little prayer.

Georgia sensed that her mother was deliberately holding back from asking the next and most important question. It was a tense moment for them all, but in the end, Nefeli herself was the one to break the silence. 'He's dead, isn't he?'

'I'm afraid so,' Hannelore replied.

'When?'

'Three years ago. It was a heart attack and it happened the day he was due to fly here. He said he wanted to see where he was stationed during the war,' Hannelore paused for a moment, 'but I now know that wasn't the reason at all.' She could barely speak from the emotion welling up inside her. 'I believe he wanted to see you.'

The thought that dredging up the past might result in a similar fate as that of Heindorf, made Georgia proceed with caution, but she could tell Hannelore's presence had ignited a flame in her mother's heart.

Hannelore took the photograph and glass dolphin out of her bag. 'These were found in his suitcase after he died — he was coming here to find you.'

Nefeli had a faraway look. 'All those years I loved him: it was as if time stood still. Fifty years and yet his shadow has always been with me, comforting me in my darkest hours.' She turned to look at Hannelore. 'You must understand that I loved my husband too… but your father was the one who really stole my heart, and the memories of those few short weeks during the summer of '44 has given me the strength to carry on. Yes, our time was brief, but you never forget a love like that, my dear. It is with you every waking moment, and at night it comes to you in a dream, caressing your soul and breathing life into you so that you can carry on.' She smiled, the one side of her face, glowing with happiness at the memory, the other, frozen in time through scarring. 'I saw him everywhere: in the brightest star, in the birds that came to my window — he was there. After a love like that, you can endure anything life throws at you.'

Nefeli paused, lost in her memories, before continuing. 'But he was not mine and I knew it from the start. Fate brought us together, and fate took him away. It was not meant to be. I knew he was married and in the end I accepted God would not look kindly on us.'

Hannelore glanced sideways at Georgia. She saw how religious Nefeli was and how circumstances really had thrown them together despite the outcome.

'My Papa never spoke about you, but my mother knew he loved someone else,' Hannelore said. 'He was a good man and tried to do what he thought was right, but sometimes that is not always the right thing to do. Like my mother, I believe you were his real love too, and from the brief time I've spent with you and your daughter, I am happy you did find each other, but there is something I need to know. How did it happen and what happened that made you separate?'

Georgia asked her mother if she wanted to continue. She realised herself, that there were parts of the story she didn't know either. Over the next hour, Nefeli told Hannelore about the storm and about finding her father washed up on the beach.

'At the time I never thought he would live, and if I am honest with you, I'm not even sure I wanted him to live. He was the enemy. After the Italians surrendered a few months earlier, there were terrible battles for our islands. As you know, the Germans won, but it came at a huge cost. Our *andartes* did what they could to fight them and many died, including some of my closest friends. All the same, as a woman of conscience, I felt God would not look kindly on me if I knowingly let a man die. So Georgia and I hid him here.' She glanced at Georgia. 'It was our secret.'

She also added that when he became conscious, he attempted to leave but was too ill and returned to the house and that it was

217

during those few days they realised they'd fallen in love with each other.

'It was like a tidal wave — unstoppable,' Nefeli said. 'But something happened and the villagers turned against me.' She told her about Konstantinos and how they blamed her for his death. The look on Hannelore's face told her she was having a hard time comprehending the situation. 'I don't expect you to understand. In those days, the villagers had different ideas.'

'Is that how you got the scars?' Hannelore asked. 'When they came for you?'

Nefeli nodded. 'I never really had time to say goodbye to your father. All I knew is that I had to get him away or the villagers would kill him. The plan was always that he would leave from Aphrodite's Cove,' she pointed in the direction of the sea, 'and attract the attention of a passing German patrol boat in the morning, but the villagers were also scouring the coast that night and they would have found him.' She turned to Georgia. 'That's when I told him to head to the cave and take the caique. It was also when I gave him the necklace. The photograph I gave him earlier, when I gave him back his belongings, which I'd hidden.'

Georgia was also having a hard time taking it all in. 'But I thought the gate to the cave entrance was always locked,' she said.

'I showed him where your father's caique was hidden the night before and purposely left it unlocked. I think there was something inside me warning me he was in grave danger. It was a feeling I had at the time. The night the villagers came, we parted ways at the cove. I knew that if they saw me, they would take their anger out on me and that would give him time to escape. He was to take the boat and escape to Kos.'

'Mama, did you know he made it to Kos? You were unconscious for a few days and we thought we'd lose you. You never spoke of…' Georgia was suddenly conscious of the way she referred to Martin in the presence of his daughter. 'You never spoke of him again.'

Nefeli looked at her daughter. 'It was better to leave things as they were. What good would it have done?' She continued with her story. 'We were taken by boat to Kalymnos by the friend who saved us — Dimitri the fisherman and his wife, Toula. It's his son who runs the donkey excursions to Chora. Dimitri asked a cousin there to keep us safe. He and his wife were good people, but little did we know at the time that we would spend the next few years there. About a month later, I was told a man was looking for me. At first I feared it was one of the villagers from Chora, but the family in Kalymnos said he was from Kos. He didn't give his name and neither did he ask for me by name. He merely said he was looking for the lady who ran the Blue Dolphin taverna on the other island. Naturally, the friends were suspicious but he managed to convince them it was important and he meant me no ill will, so they arranged for me to meet him in a *kafeneio* on the seafront. Imagine my surprise when I saw it was the same man who had dropped the German/Greek dictionary — the translator, Christos Grivas.

'It was an even bigger surprise when I saw he was carrying the leather satchel I gave Martin to carry his few possessions when he left. The meeting was brief. "This is for you," he said, handing me the bag. "The gentleman that gave it to me said to tell you it was a sign." Can you imagine my joy? I knew then that he had made it to Kos.

'"You are a hard lady to find," Grivas said. "I went to the island and saw what happened to the taverna. After a few enquires, I found out you were on Kalymnos." I asked him if he would see the man again and he said no. He'd been sent to Rhodes. The man whispered that there was something in the satchel that would help me, but I was not to say anything to anyone or I might find myself in trouble.'

Georgia's eyes widened. 'It's the first I heard of it. I don't recall you meeting with anyone.'

'At the time I didn't even know if it was a trap. All I could think of at that moment was my absolute joy on hearing he'd escaped. Grivas also told me that there were two men from the island who had been imprisoned in Kos and that for some reason which he wasn't made aware of, they were released and allowed to go back home just days before they were due to be executed. I found out soon after that it was the mayor and the schoolteacher and that it must have been due to Martin's intervention. Of course I had no proof at the time though. It was just a feeling.'

'What was in the bag?' Georgia asked.

'Money — lots of it — Drachmas, Reichmarks, and American dollars.' Georgia and Hannelore exchanged glances. They were too shocked to speak. 'I put it aside until after the war. I couldn't let anyone know I had it in case I was branded a traitor. When we returned to the island a few years later, I used it to rebuild the new taverna.' There was pause. 'Maybe now you will understand why I believed he was always still with me.'

'And there was no letter with it?' Georgia asked.

'No. Having the money was dangerous enough, but a letter would really have compromised me. Martin knew that. A month later the Germans surrendered and I never knew until now if he survived the war.'

There was a long, awkward silence while the enormity of this latest revelation sank in. In the end it was Hannelore who broke the silence. She commented on how beautiful Nefeli looked in the photograph.

'It's not hard to see why my father fell in love with you.'

Nefeli touched her scarred face. 'Maybe, but the villagers made sure no-one would ever look at me again. It was probably for the best that he never returned. I think it would have destroyed him. Sometimes it's better to leave things as they are.'

Georgia looked at her watch and said they must leave or she would miss the boat. Hannelore said she had something else she wanted to give Nefeli. She took another photograph from her bag. It was of her father in his youth.

'It was taken when he joined the Luftwaffe.'

When Nefeli looked at his face, her eyes lit up. 'That is how I remember him. He was most handsome.'

'I want you to have it,' Hannelore said.

'Are you quite sure, my dear?'

'Quite sure. I know he would want that too.'

Nefeli's eyes glistened with tears. 'I can see you are a good girl. Your parents raised you well.'

It was hard for Hannelore to say goodbye. There was so much about the woman her father had loved that she wanted to know, yet she felt a great weight had been lifted — for all of them. Driving back along the road, Hannelore took in the beautiful coastline and tried to imagine what took place that fateful night he arrived — and departed. She fought back the tears, but this time they were tears of joy.

By the time they reached the jetty, the other tourists were already boarding the boat. Hannelore embraced Georgia and thanked her for her kindness. Georgia watched the boat leave, waving until it disappeared out of sight around the cove. Stephanos came over and stood by her side.

'Was she a friend?' he asked. 'You seemed pretty close.'

Georgia found herself becoming quite emotional. 'You could say that,' she said, choking back the tears.

When she returned to the house, she found Nefeli sitting outside with the dog at her feet. She was dressed in her best Sunday clothes and had fixed her hair neatly into a bun. She also wore her necklace with the glass dolphin.

'I want you to take me to the church of the Panagia Thalassini,' she said.

The sun was beginning to sink over the horizon by the time they got there. As usual, it was empty and the door unlocked. Georgia said she would wait outside to give her mother time alone. Nefeli lit a candle and placed in on the altar in front of the icon of the Virgin as she had done so often in the past, except that this time, she placed Martin's photograph next to the icon. She spent several minutes in prayer, thanking the Virgin for looking after him all these years.

During the drive back, Georgia said she was sorry if she made life hard for her all those years ago. 'I really had no idea that you loved him so much, Mama. Please forgive me.'

'There's nothing to forgive,' Nefeli replied. 'Nothing at all. A love like that is rare. It burns forever in your heart, drives us to madness and refuses to be extinguished. I endured it all and now I feel free of grief.'

She turned her eyes momentarily towards the golden sunset over the Aegean and Georgia saw a peacefulness on her face that she had not seen in years. It was as if a weight had been lifted.

'And now,' Nefeli said, after a few moments of silence. 'Let's go home and finish that bottle of wine. It's a pity to leave it.'

Postscript

THE STORY IS set on an unnamed island in the Dodecanese group of islands in the southeastern Aegean Sea. "Dodecanese" (τα Δωδεκάνησα), means "The Twelve Islands" but actually comprises of fifteen major islands (Agathonisi, Astypalaia, Chalki, Kalymnos, Karpathos, Kasos, Kastellorizo, Kos, Lipsi, Leros, Nisyros, Patmos, Rhodes, Symi, and Tilos) and 93 smaller islets. These islands form part of the group known as the "Southern Sporades".

I purposely chose not to give the island a name and to simply refer to it as "the island" because although the story is fictional, I did not want to cast a particular known island in a bad light, but the events which took place would not have been uncommon throughout certain areas of Greece at the time. Arranged marriages by matchmakers were common, even into the 1970's, and were an important part of societal attitudes. Furthermore, families and villages were torn apart because of people who were dishonoured in one way or another — love interests and business being the main causes, but merely stealing someone's goat could also cause vendettas resulting in death.

In the 1940's, village life in Greece was still extremely culturally sensitive, and it was common for a widow to wear black after her husband died, even if the woman was still young. The fact that the free-spirited Nefeli purposely chose to stop wearing black would have been seen as a sign to the matchmakers that it was time to suggest a new husband for her.

The other reason for the story being set in this area was that during WWII, the Dodecanese Islands played a strategic part of the Allied campaign in Greece. When Italy joined the Axis Powers, the Dodecanese was used as a naval staging area for their invasion of Crete in 1941. After Italy surrendered in September 1943, the islands briefly became a battleground between the Germans and Allied forces, including the Italians. The Germans won in the Dodecanese Campaign, and although they were driven out of mainland Greece in 1944, the islands remained occupied until the end of the war in 1945. After the Italians capitulated, the Germans set about ridding the islands of their Jewish population. 6,000 were deported and killed although many survived by escaping to the nearby Turkey. On 8 May 1945 the German garrison commander Otto Wagener surrendered the islands to the British on Rhodes handing over 5,000 German and 600 Italian military personnel.

X. Fliegerkorps — the10th Air Corps — was a formation of the German Luftwaffe which specialised in coastal operations during WWII. It was formed 2 October 1939, in Hamburg from the 10. Flieger-Division. The Corps was crucial in securing air superiority and German victory during the Dodecanese Campaign. It was renamed to *Kommandierender General der Deutschen Luftwaffe in Griechenland* (commanding general of the German Luftwaffe in Greece) in March 1944 and disbanded on 5 September 1944 with the withdrawal of German forces from the country.

Kakavia

Greek Fisherman's Soup

Ingredients

- 1 kilo whole white fish such as red snapper, cod, monkfish, mullet, or any smaller fish if available. Scale and clean, but leave the head on. This adds taste.
- 8 cups of water (preferably sea water if cooking near the sea)
- ¼ cup olive oil
- 1 small onion, finely chopped
- 2 celery stalks, diced (You can also use ½ cup of chopped celery leaves if they are young)
- 2-3 garlic cloves, crushed
- 3 potatoes, peeled and diced
- 2-3 chopped tomatoes.
- 1 chopped carrot.
- Saffron
- 1 Bay leaf
- Fresh thyme
- Salt and pepper.
- 2 lemons
- 2 tablespoons fresh chopped parsley

Method

1. Place the water and fish into a pot and season lightly with salt. Bring to a boil and simmer for 30 minutes or until fish is cooked
2. Transfer the fish to a platter and strain the broth to catch any fish bones. Discard the bones.
3. Clean the pot and return the broth.
4. Add the onion, celery, tomatoes, carrot, potatoes, garlic to the pot.
5. Add the olive oil, saffron, bay leaf and thyme sprigs. Season with salt and pepper.
6. Cook over medium heat until potatoes are soft.
7. At this point you can add clams, mussels or shrimps, etc. and continue cooking until cooked through.
8. Pull the meat from the cooked fish into chunks and add it to the soup at the last minute.
9. Taste and adjust the seasoning if needed.
10. Garnish with parsley and serve with lemon wedges and crusty bread.

NOTE: Greeks grow celery just for the celery leaves. It gives a delicate taste to soups. Some people fry the onion and celery first, but it is common to add the olive oil after the other ingredients have been added. The olive oil tends to emulsify the soup.

Also by the Author

The Secret of the Grand Hôtel du Lac
Conspiracy of Lies
The Poseidon Network
Code Name Camille
The Embroiderer
The Carpet Weaver of Uşak
Seraphina's Song

WEBSITE:
https://www.kathryngauci.com/

To sign up to my newsletter,
please visit my website and fill out the form.

The Secret of the Grand Hôtel du Lac

Amazon Best Seller in German
and French Literature (Kindle Store)

From USA TODAY Bestselling Author, Kathryn Gauci, comes an unforgettable story of love, hope and betrayal, and of the power of human endurance during history's darkest days.

Inspired by true events, The Secret of the Grand Hôtel du Lac is a gripping and emotional portrait of wartime France... a true-page-turner.

"Dripping with suspense on every page" — JJ Toner

"SOMETIME DURING THE early hours of the morning, he awoke again, this time with a start. He was sure he heard a noise outside. It sounded like a twig snapping. Under normal circumstances it would have meant nothing, but in the silence of the forest every sound was magnified. There it was again. This time it was closer and his instinct told him it wasn't the wolves. He reached for his gun and quietly looked out through the window. The moon was on the wane, wrapped in the soft gauze of snowfall and it wasn't easy to see. Maybe it was a fox, or even a deer. Then he heard it again, right outside the door. He cocked his gun, pressed his body flat against the wall next to the door, and waited. The room was in total darkness and his senses were heightened. After a few minutes, he heard the soft click of the door latch."

February 1944. Preparations for the D-Day invasion are well

advanced. When contact with Belvedere, one of the Resistance networks in the Jura region of Eastern France, is lost, Elizabeth Maxwell, is sent back to the region to find the head of the network, her husband Guy Maxwell.

It soon becomes clear that the network has been betrayed. An RAF airdrop of supplies was ambushed by the Gestapo, and many members of the Resistance have been killed.

Surrounded on all sides by the brutal Gestapo and the French Milice, and under constant danger of betrayal, Elizabeth must unmask the traitor in their midst, find her husband, and help him to rebuild Belvedere in time for SOE operations in support of D-Day.

Amazon Reviews

"Enthralling. This is a page-turner." Marina Osipova

"A historical fiction masterpiece." Amazon Top 100 Customer Review

"Incredible book." Turgay Cevikogullari

"Author paints wonderful pictures with her words." Avidreader

"Great storytelling of important historical time." Luv2read

"Complex characters and a compelling storyline." Pamela Allegretto

"An SOE mission to German occupied France fraught with danger" Induna

Conspiracy of Lies

A powerful account of one woman's struggle to balance her duty to her country and a love she knows will ultimately end in tragedy. *Which would you choose?*

1940. The Germans are about to enter Paris, Claire Bouchard flees for England. Two years later she is sent back to work alongside the Resistance.

Working undercover as a teacher in Brittany, Claire accidentally befriends the wife of the German Commandant of Rennes and the blossoming friendship is about to become a dangerous mission.

Knowing thousands of lives depend on her actions, Claire begins a double life as a Gestapo Commandant's mistress in order to retrieve vital information for the Allies, but ghosts from her past make the deception more painful than she could have imagined.

A time of horror, yet amongst so much strength and love Conspiracy of Lies takes us on a journey through occupied France, from the picturesque villages of rural Brittany to the glittering dinner parties of the Nazi elite.

Amazon Reviews

"My heart! What a fabulous story." Amazon Top Customer

"Gripping and Charismatic." B. Gaskell-Denvil

"This novel should be made into a movie." Wendy J. Dunn

"Beware, this story will grip you." Helen Hollick for *A Discovered Diamond*

"Well-written and emotional." Pauline for *A Chill with a Book Readers' Award*

The Poseidon Network

A mesmerising, emotional espionage thriller that no fan of WWII fiction will want to miss.

"One never knows where fate will take us. Cairo taught me that. Expect the unexpected. Little did I realise when I left London that I would walk out of one nightmare into another."

1943. SOE agent Larry Hadley leaves Cairo for German and Italian occupied Greece. His mission is to liaise with the Poseidon network under the leadership of the White Rose.

It's not long before he finds himself involved with a beautiful and intriguing woman whose past is shrouded in mystery. In a country where hardship, destruction and political instability threaten to split the Resistance, and terror and moral ambiguity live side by side, Larry's instincts tell him something is wrong.

After the devastating massacre in a small mountain village by the Wehrmacht, combined with new intelligence concerning the escape networks, he is forced to confront the likelihood of a traitor in their midst. But who is it?

Time is running out and he must act before the network is blown. The stakes are high.

From the shadowy souks and cocktail parties of Cairo's elite to the mountains of Greece, Athens, the Aegean Islands, and Turkey, The Poseidon Network, is an unforgettable cat-and-mouse portrait of wartime that you will not want to put down.

Amazon Reviews

"This Historical Novel is alive." Pamporos

"Excellent novel about the Greek Resistance." Vet 49

"An intoxicating book that keeps you turning the pages." Kellie

"Meticulously researched and compelling." Amazon Top Customer

The Embroiderer

A richly woven saga set against the mosques and minarets of Asia Minor and the ruins of ancient Athens. Extravagant, inventive, emotionally sweeping, The Embroiderer is a tale that travellers and those who seek culture and oriental history will love

1822: During one of the bloodiest massacres of The Greek War of Independence, a child is born to a woman of legendary beauty in the Byzantine monastery of Nea Moni on the Greek island of Chios. The subsequent decades of bitter struggle between Greeks and Turks simmer to a head when the Greek army invades Turkey in 1919. During this time, Dimitra Lamartine arrives in Smyrna and gains fame and fortune as an embroiderer to the elite of Ottoman society. However it is her grand-daughter Sophia, who takes the business to great heights only to see their world come crashing down with the outbreak of The Balkan Wars, 1912-13. In 1922, Sophia begins a new life in Athens but when the Germans invade Greece during WWII, the memory of a dire prophecy once told to her grandmother about a girl with flaming red hair begins to haunt her with devastating consequences.

1972: Eleni Stephenson is called to the bedside of her dying aunt in Athens. In a story that rips her world apart, Eleni discovers the chilling truth behind her family's dark past plunging her into the shadowy world of political intrigue, secret societies and espionage where families and friends are torn apart and where a belief in superstition simmers just below the surface.

The Embroiderer is not only a vivid, cinematic tale of romance, glamour, and political turmoil, it is also a gripping saga of love and loss, hope and despair, and of the extraordinary courage of women in the face of adversity.

Amazon Reviews

"The Embroiderer is a beautifully embroidered book." Jel Cel

"Stunning." Abzorba the Greek

"Remarkable… even through the tears." Marva

"A lyrical, enthralling journey in Greek history." Effrosyne Moschoudi

"A great book and addictive page-turner." Lena

"The needle and the pen create a masterpiece." Alan Hamilton

"The Embroiderer reveals the futility of way and the resilience of the human spirit." Pamporos

"A towering achievement" Marjory McGinn

The Carpet Weaver of Uşak

A haunting story of a deep friendship between two women, one Greek, one Turk. A friendship that transcends an era of mistrust, and fear, long after the wars have ended.

"Springtime and early summer are always beautiful in Anatolia. Hardy winter crocuses, blooming in their thousands, are followed by blue muscari which adorn the meadows like glorious sapphires on a silk carpet."

Aspasia and Saniye are friends from childhood. They share their secrets and joy, helping each other in times of trouble.

When WWI breaks, the news travels to the village, but the locals have no idea how it will affect their lives.

When the war ends the Greeks come to the village, causing havoc, burning houses and shooting Turks. The residents regard each other with suspicion. Their world has turned upside down, but some of the old friendships survive, despite the odds.

But the Greeks are finally defeated, and the situation changes once more, forcing the Greeks to leave the country. Yet, the friendship between the villagers still continues.

Many years later, in Athens, Christophorus tells his grandson, and his daughter, Elpida, the missing parts of the story, and what he had to leave behind in Asia Minor.

A story of love, friendship, and loss; a tragedy that affects the lives of many on both sides of the Aegean, and their struggle to survive under new circumstances, as casualties of a war beyond their control.

If you enjoyed Louis de Berniers' *Birds Without Wings* then you will love Kathryn Gauci's *The Carpet Weaver of Usak*. "As she weaves her poignant story and characters with the expert hands of a carpet weaver."

Amazon Reviews

"An unforgettable atmospheric read." Amazon Top Reviewer

"So beautifully written." Elizabeth Moore

"Broken homes, broken lives, and lasting friendships." Sebnem Sanders

"Hooked from page one!" Francis Broun

Seraphina's Song

"If I knew then, dear reader, what I know now, I should have turned on my heels and left. But I stood transfixed on the beautiful image of Seraphina. In that moment my fate was sealed."

Dionysos Mavroulis is a man without a future: a man who embraces destiny and risks everything for love.

A refugee from Asia Minor, he escapes Smyrna in 1922 disguised as an old woman. Alienated and plagued by feelings of remorse, he spirals into poverty and seeks solace in the hashish dens around Piraeus.

Hitting rock bottom, he meets Aleko, an accomplished bouzouki player. Recognising in the impoverished refugee a rare musical talent, Aleko offers to teach him the bouzouki.

Dionysos' hope for the future is further fuelled when he meets Seraphina — the singer with the voice of a nightingale — at Papazoglou's Taverna. From the moment he lays eyes on her, his fate is sealed.

Set in Piraeus in the 1920's and 30's, Seraphina's Song is a haunting and compelling story of hope and despair, and of a love stronger than death.

A haunting and compelling story of hope and despair, and of a love stronger than death.

Amazon Reviews

"Cine noir meets Greek tragedy, played out with a Depression era realism. Gauci creates in this novel the smoke, songs and music of Papazoglou's tavern so convincingly one can almost hear the strings through the tobacco-fuelled murk. " Helen Hollick *A Discovered Diamond*

"A very beautiful novel, I couldn't put it down." Pauline *A Chill with a Book Award*

"A book like no other." Jo-Anne Himmelman

"Dark and emotionally charged." David Baird

"The Passion That Ignited Greek History." Viviane Chrystal

"Where there is love, there is hope." Janet Ellis

Code Name Camille

Originally part of the USA Today runaway bestseller, The Darkest Hour Anthology: WWII Tales of Resistance. **Code Name Camille, now a standalone novella.**

1940: Paris under Nazi occupation. A gripping tale of resistance, suspense and love.

When the Germans invade France, twenty-one-year-old Nathalie Fontaine is living a quiet life in rural South-West France. Within months, she heads for Paris and joins the Resistance as a courier helping to organise escape routes. But Paris is fraught with danger. When several escapes are foiled by the Gestapo, the network suspects they are compromised.

Nathalie suspects one person, but after a chance encounter with a stranger who provides her with an opportunity to make a little extra money by working as a model for a couturier known to be sympathetic to the Nazi cause, her suspicions are thrown into doubt.

Using her work in the fashionable rue du Faubourg Saint-Honoré, she uncovers information vital to the network, but at the same time steps into a world of treachery and betrayal which threatens to bring them all undone.

Time is running out and the Gestapo is closing in.

Code Name Camille is a story of courage and resilience that fans of The Nightingale and The Alice Network will love.

Author Biography

KATHRYN GAUCI WAS born in Leicestershire, England, and studied textile design at Loughborough College of Art and later at Kidderminster College of Art and Design where she specialised in carpet design and technology. After graduating, Kathryn spent a year in Vienna, Austria before moving to Greece where she worked as a carpet designer in Athens for six years. There followed another brief period in New Zealand before eventually settling in Melbourne, Australia.

Before turning to writing full-time, Kathryn ran her own textile design studio in Melbourne for over fifteen years, work which she enjoyed tremendously as it allowed her the luxury of travelling worldwide, often taking her off the beaten track and exploring other cultures. *The Embroiderer* is her first novel; a culmination of those wonderful years of design and travel, and especially of those glorious years in her youth living and working in Greece.

Since then, she has gone on to become an international bestselling author. *Code Name Camille*, written as part of *The Darkest Hour Anthology: WWII Tales of Resistance*, became a *USA TODAY* **Bestseller** in the first week of publication, and The Secret of the Grand Hotel du Lac became an **Amazon Best Seller in both German Literature and French Literature. (Kindle Store)**

Made in the USA
Las Vegas, NV
11 February 2022

43707832R00142